TALES OF
CHINKAPIN CREEK

JEAN AYER

Some of these stories have appeared in *Appalachian Heritage*, *Confrontation*, and other literary magazines.

ISBN: 061545271X
ISBN-13: 9780615452715

Library of Congress Control Number: 2011903263

Mama and Papa

CONTENTS

Acknowledgments

I'd like to thank my son Bob Ayer for improving every inch of these stories, and the same goes for my good friend and fellow West Virginian Kevin Meredith. My wonderfully gifted sister Ann Van Saun and my talented nephew Kyle Van Saun provided amazing insights and suggestions.

I'm also indebted to the following writers, aka "The Group": Myriam Chapman, Judi Culbertson, Teresa Giordano, Adele Glimm, Tom House, Eleanor Hyde, Harriet LaBarre, Elisabeth Jakab, Carol Pepper, Maureen Sladen, and Marcia Slatkin.

For my mother

Introduction

When my mother turned seventy in 1965, I asked her to write about her life. She was born in the part of Virginia that became West Virginia during the War Between the States in a house that had belonged to her family for nine generations. The farmhouse and land were owned first by her mother's family. When the place fell to a childless old bachelor, her father's family bought him out. The house's exterior walls were a yard thick, with a core of chestnut logs, and the interior plaster was made of horsehair and lime. Deeds from her father's safe are dated from the 1700s. Many were on parchment, and some were signed by Lighthorse Harry Lee.

In my childhood, this farm was considered modern; however, it operated pretty much in the old frontier style. Meat, wool, leather, soap, wheat, corn, flax, broomcorn, and sorghum were some of its produce.

In my mother's time, there were reunions of Confederate veterans from the easternmost counties of the relatively new State of West Virginia and adjacent western counties of Virginia. They met yearly at a reunion ground five miles from her family's farm.

Uncle Edward, far left. Papa, second from right.

UNCLE EDWARD

The morning my father was born in November 1865 his brothers assembled a makeshift a platform outside Grandma's ground-floor bedroom window to watch him arrive. Uncle Walter was seven, Uncle Edward five, Uncle Hugh four, and Uncle Pent barely three. Their platform consisted of a rain barrel and two or three old chestnut rails. Just as their suspicions were about to be confirmed as to where babies came from, it collapsed. The neighbor woman helping Grandma rushed out and managed to collar Edward.

"What do you have to say for yourself, Edward Wister?" she demanded.

"Pa said he was going to add a porch on this side," he said. "We were just getting a start on it to surprise him."

My father loved this story, but I found it hard to believe. How could the brave five-year-old in that story have grown up to be the dull, totally humorless man my brothers and I knew as our Uncle Edward?

The Uncle Edward *we* knew, the *Reverend* Edward Wister, arrived every summer from Baltimore, two hundred miles away, driving an aged, roan mare and a dusty, old buggy. He had followed a roundabout itinerary that included *many* stopovers in the homes of his Methodist minister colleagues. This saved him the cost of lodging.

In Maryland, Uncle Edward stopped at Ellicott City, Mount Airy, Frederick, and Boonsboro; in Virginia, at

Winchester, Capon Bridge, and Augusta; and in West Virginia, at Moorefield and a town called Vestal, nineteen miles from our farm. He arrived painfully sunburned, with his nose peeling, sometimes even bleeding. He tossed his reins and his plug hat to my brothers. At the sound of his arrival, they had run out to meet him. He eased himself stiffly down from the buggy seat. Then he turned himself around to pick up his Bible and tucked it under his arm. He said not a word to my brothers or me. No hello. Not even a glance in our direction. He just headed for the house.

"Well, Edward, here you are," Papa greeted him coolly.

Mama touched her fingertips to the collar of her dress. "Well, Edward," she said.

Grandpa and Grandma Wister, Uncle Edward's own parents, seemed oddly quiet. He received their greetings as his due. Without a word, he then proceeded through the house to the front porch. He sat in the best chair. He took from his pocket a small black notebook, a black hard-rubber fountain pen, and a pocket-size Bible concordance. He then set about the job that would occupy him the whole two months of his visit—composing his sermons for the coming year. Grandpa and Papa, who hadn't seen him since the summer before, also moved to the porch. They sat at the opposite end from Uncle Edward, discussing politics and farming until our hired girl came through the house ringing her bell for supper.

As a minister, Uncle Edward had the honor of saying grace at meals. For a short, freckled, skinny, inconspicuous-looking man, he had a surprisingly powerful voice. First, he blessed us, each one, by name. Then he blessed his flock in Baltimore. He blessed his preacher friends who had put him up on his long, long drive. He blessed the food on the table. When he finally finished his blessings, the meal was cold. He ate his cold ham and congealing milk gravy, never joining in the general conversation. The rest of us were still eating when, abruptly, he rose and left the room, with no word of excuse, no farewell, no thanks, nor any compliments to the cooks.

When bedtime rolled around, Papa escorted him from the porch into the parlor to join us for a bedtime hymn. He led us again in evening prayer, another endless session.

Grandma Wister darned his socks. She stitched up holes in his pockets. She turned the collars of his shirts. He had brought all these clothes with him, a year's supply, just for her.

He couldn't write legibly, so he drafted us children into doing his correspondence. Following his instructions, we wrote in the normal direction across penny postcards until we had filled them up. Then we gave the cards a quarter turn and wrote over our original script, creating grids of writing that saved him the cost of more postcards.

We became so used to having him underfoot that it always came as a surprise when, one morning at breakfast, he said dryly, "Well, I must be on my way." We children were sent to the barn for his buggy and mare. She was sleek from two months of living on our oats and fodder and the rich grass in our pastures. We were then sent upstairs to bring down his grips.

Papa and Grandpa shook Uncle Edward's hand. Mama contributed a civil, but uncharacteristically cool "Good-bye, Edward." Then off he went, retracing his dusty, circuitous, weeks-long route back to Baltimore.

Sometime in the spring of 1906, Mama was sorting through our canvas mail sack when she came upon one of Uncle Edward's postcards. She placed it, unread, on the big oak table for Papa to find. He, too, avoided it. In Baltimore, our uncle had no young relatives to write for him, so it was hard, sometimes impossible, to decipher his negligent scrawl. One day, Papa got around to puzzling it out.

Startled, he turned to Mama. "Carrie, listen to this: 'Dear all, Was married to Grace Kunstmesser of prominent Baltimore family on the seventh of April Anno Domini 1906. Grace is a lady and a musician. She has never done housework like the women we have known. She has always had a parlor with an organ. She and I arrive July first.'"

In those days, the title "lady" had to be earned. My mother considered herself, and the women in her family, to be ladies. She was making every effort to raise my sisters and me to be ladies, including teaching us to play the organ.

Dr. Sam Hunter cautioned Mama, for the sake of her back, not to climb stairs while she was pregnant. She and Papa then slept in the parlor where the organ was.

She said, "Jack, if your mother and I can do without a parlor, I expect this Grace can, too."

The day arrived when the familiar old buggy appeared on our farm lane. Our new aunt wore a beautiful dark traveling suit and wide-brimmed leghorn hat with a huge, fiery-red silk poppy on its crown.

Ola, a young hired girl, whispered, "She'll never get the road dust out of that suit."

Uncle Edward tossed my brother his plug hat and the mare's reins then eased himself down from the buggy. Tucking his Bible under his arm, he turned to hand down his bride. In a furry voice with a catch in it, our new aunt addressed my brothers and me.

"Children, I'm your Aunt Grace," she said. From that moment, our hearts were hers.

Mama and Aunt Grace turned out to have much in common. Both were young and married to older men, and both were beautiful. Aunt Grace told Mama that she had once been fat. Her father, a rich wholesale grocer, had sent her to a place in rural Maryland for a "cure."

"I lost so much weight!" she said with a giggle. "And guess what? Eddie was the first man who ever looked at me."

Eddie. Mama had never heard her brother-in-law called such a name. She, too, giggled.

At bedtime, Mama gave Aunt Grace the honor of accompanying us in a hymn. Aunt Grace pulled out the old reed organ's ivory stops, pumped up the bellows, and struck the first notes. Mama's eyes mischievously met Papa's; she herself was a much better musician.

Because Uncle Edward brought us Aunt Grace, we forgave his transgressions.

Grandpa Wister died that year and, soon afterward, so did Grandma Wister. Uncle Edward brought Aunt Grace back to West Virginia for their funerals. Through the years, letters arrived from Aunt Grace, written in her large, round hand on thick, creamy paper, with her engraved scarlet monogram, "GKW." She used only one side of the sheet and left scandalously wide, wasteful margins. She sent us children extravagant presents: a gold locket with a tiny diamond in it for me, a gold chain for my sister Bess, and books and colorful cast-iron penny banks for my brothers. She sent us boxes of glossy ribbon candy, chocolate nonpareils, spice drops, and licorice whips.

One February afternoon around 1909, a small, smart bay mare came high-stepping up our lane pulling a road cart, not a common vehicle on a working farm. It had no top and room for only one passenger. No roads were paved then, and February was no season to travel. The little mare, with a white blaze on her forehead and four white socks, was spattered liberally with red mud, but she moved like an animal that knew her value.

The driver, swathed in black oilskins, made a gesture we children recognized: He tossed us the reins—it was our Uncle Edward!

His first words to Papa were, "How do you like the mare? She's a Texas pony, Jack, a natural pacer. You would do well to ask why I drove her all this distance."

A fine drizzle, which had threatened all day, began in earnest. Uncle Edward's oilskin coat glistened.

"A rig like this has no use in a town like Baltimore. I made a mistake when I bought her. I thought of Ki Huffman. Ki'll give me a good price."

Ki Huffman was a notorious horse dealer in the town of Minerva, nineteen miles from our farm.

We wondered at Uncle Edward's unusual out-of-season visit, the unusual vehicle, the pretty little mare, and especially his volubility.

After Uncle Edward had gone up to bed, Mama challenged Papa. "You can't let that little mare go to Ki Huffman," she said.

The next day Papa made Uncle Edward an offer, which he accepted. Uncle Edward then caught the stage back to Baltimore.

We christened her "Lady May," and I discovered the pleasures of riding a pacing horse. At twelve years old, I thought it was like sitting astride a child's toy rocking horse.

The mud in the lanes dried up, pussy willows budded, maple trees in the river bottom turned red, and Mama's forsythia burst into golden bloom. Paris Finch, a middle-aged man who worked for us, came stomping grimly up to the kitchen door and asked for a word with Papa.

"That mare your brother sold you is heavey," Paris told him.

Horses are subject to a distressing ailment, which can lie dormant, as asthma does in humans, until pollen or some other irritant triggers it. It's called "heaves."

"*That*'s why your brother brought her in February," Paris said.

I remember Lady May standing knee deep in lush new grass, her beautiful, intelligent eyes fixed on our other horses in the distance. She seemed to ask, *Why am I here and they over there?* Papa had moved her to the log stable, separate from the big barn where we kept the other horses. Besides the usual oats, corn, and fodder, he gave her molasses. Once the pollen season was well over, he turned her onto grass.

She became my horse. I rode her to school, to visit Grandma Cody, on excursions with Papa, and to play with my friend Maud Flood.

In 1912, Uncle Edward and Aunt Grace paid us another surprise visit. Aunt Grace must have insisted on the trip. I couldn't resist telling her everything about Lady May.

The story seemed to surprise and displease her.

"You don't mean to say Eddie drove that little mare all the way down here just to cheat you?" she said.

The next day, Uncle Edward looked chastened.

"That's not my Texas pony, is it?" he asked, making an obvious effort at lightness.

"It *was* your Texas pony, Edward," Mama told him grimly.

As Aunt Grace grew older, she gave up curling her hair. She had two children and gained weight with each. She eventually became as fat as she must have been before her father sent her away for the cure.

I finished school in our village and then went away to boarding school and junior college. Afterward, I taught school in Monroe County, married, and moved with my husband to the other side of the state. Meanwhile, Lady May became Mama's horse.

Several years after Uncle Edward died, I received a letter from Aunt Grace. Tucked inside was one of Uncle Edward's postcards. She'd found it in his bureau drawer. It was one of the many he'd dictated to me, but somehow failed to mail. Written in my own careful schoolgirl script, the note had a few final lines, in his scribble, across mine: "Am staying with my folks here, fine old homestead, a showplace. My brother is a leader in his community. He has a beautiful wife and fine children. A pleasure to come here to rest from my labors in the Lord's vineyards." Uncle Edward had signed it, "EW, per Nellie Wister, Aug. 5, 1904."

That summer I went home to visit Mama. Papa had died. I took Uncle Edward's card with me. Mama and I sat by the sitting room window in about the same positions and in the same chairs as where she and Aunt Grace had spent long afternoons. I watched her read the postcard, then, sighing, let it fall to her lap.

The walnut-case clock above our heads struck the half hour. Late-afternoon sunlight slanted across the room, filtered by the foliage of the goose plum tree. Through the open window, we faintly heard the desultory conversation of my brother and my husband. They sat on the porch where Uncle Edward used to sit, composing his sermons.

A sparkle appeared in Mama's eyes. "Good old Eddie," she said. "I don't miss him a bit."

Montani Semper Liberi

To understand Singleton's Gap is to understand West Virginia. Singleton's Gap is a precipitous gorge, flung up violently in prehistoric times. It has thousand-foot cliffs, jagged rocks, unsure footing, rattlesnakes, copperheads, bears, bobcats, wolves, panthers, and Scotsmen. These Scots are descended from survivors of Oliver Cromwell's depredations in the Hebrides. Also in the Gap are descendants of Hessian soldiers. Deserters from the British Colonial Army, these mercenaries felt ill-used by the British.

No one knows when the Gap's inhabitants began to brew corn liquor, but that industry made the place extremely dangerous for outsiders. In the early 1900s, my father held the post of collector of internal revenue for the six counties in West Virginia's eastern panhandle. He did not collect revenue on corn liquor. That had been tried, and the revenue collector vanished, never to be seen again.

Papa was born in the mountains. He understood the role corn liquor played in the lives of mountaineers. On the date he chose to inspect the Gap's small general store, he met Old Sinnott Singleton on the narrow iron bridge at the turnoff from the main road. Old Sinnott had met Papa's father on the bridge, and *Old Sinnot's* father had met Papa's *grand*father there. Papa and Old Sinnott threaded their way through the narrow bottleneck that stoppers the gorge. High above them, sharpshooters armed with rifles watched them pass. A contemporary of Papa's had disappeared in the gorge. His body was never found.

As Old Sinnott led Papa along a narrow creek bed, they were forced to dismount and lead their horses. Old Sinnott was so tall that, as he rode, his size-fourteen brogans nearly touched the ground.

"You and I are the long and the short of it," he told Papa, little more than half his size. Old Sinnott glanced at the wisps of vapor that curled above the ridges. "Ed Teter's woman's making a turn of apple butter," he said. "Amos Hamrick's sister's making soap."

No one made apple butter in the springtime. Someone *might* make soap. Papa smelled the sour mash, but didn't turn his head to look. He didn't want to know too much. He recalled West Virginia's state motto: *Montani Semper Liberi*, meaning "Mountaineers are always free." They rode on.

Like all rural stores in those days, the small facility that hove into sight sold yard goods, hardware, plug and loose tobacco, and snuff. Papa collected taxes on these items. Loafers, squatting on the porch, spat long streams of tobacco juice into the dust. Papa knew these men. They worked "just enough to get by," as they said. He knew their wives and children, too. He knew where they lived, as he had lent money to most of them.

"Now, Mr. Wister," one of the men said, "can we offer ye something to drink? Sassafras tea? Buttermilk? Branch water?"

They laughed. They knew Papa was a teetotaler.

Old Sinnott and his wife, Josie, had raised twenty-one children in their two-room cabin. She served Papa salt-cured side meat with cornbread and milk gravy. If it was early in the year, she served him ramps, a kind of leek that grows wild in the mountains. Papa never got ramps at home, for they have the most powerful stench imaginable, an oniony reek that lasts for days on the skin and breath. When Papa came home, Mama always said bitterly, "Jack, you've been eating *ramps*."

Old Sinnott died. His son, Big Dan, took over the job of ensuring Papa's safety in the Gap. The first time he escorted Papa to his house, Papa noticed a hole in the roof and a washtub under it to collect rainwater.

Big Dan said, "I come down through that hole when I put on the roof, but I never got around to closing it up."

Big Dan's house consisted of one room and a lean-to. Big Dan and his pretty young wife, Tildy, had three children, but only one bed. After a supper of fried side meat and hominy, Tildy put the children to bed. Once they were asleep, she moved them to a quilt on the floor. While she set the table for breakfast, Papa and Big Dan sat talking.

"You take the bed," Big Dan told Papa. He and Tildy disappeared into the lean-to. Papa assumed they had some arrangement there for sleeping, but the next morning, he found himself on the floor with the children. Big Dan and Tildy had the bed.

The next night, Papa resolved to stay awake and see how they managed to move him. But his long day in the high, thin mountain air put him soundly to sleep. The next morning, he again found himself on the floor with the children.

Old Sinnott had another son who was a famous maker and consumer of corn liquor. One day, he stumbled out into the road, shook his fist at the heavens, and shouted, "I don't believe there's a God, and I don't believe there's a hell! If there is, let Him strike me dead!" At that moment, a bolt of lightning flashed in the clear sky, and he dropped where he stood. On Papa's next visit, Big Dan, escorting him past the grave, muttered, "I reckon my brother found out if there's a hell." He spat a stream of tobacco juice into the dust.

In October, Big Dan came to work for us. He mostly cut and shucked corn, but if the weather stayed cool, he helped with other fall work. "I cain't abide hot weather," he'd say. He was even taller than Old Sinnott. When he slept in our hired-men's room, his feet hung over the end of the bed.

Mama loved the smooth, buttery color of the tongue-and-groove pine walls where Big Dan slept. They never needed daubing or whitewashing, as did plaster walls.

After Big Dan had finished his fall work, our young hired girl went into his room to change the bedding. She found the wall, at the foot of his bed, discolored with dark streaks. With a corner of her apron, she rubbed the streaks then sniffed the cloth.

"He's been a-laying in that bed a-spitting tobacco juice on the walls," she told Mama. She and Mama scoured the beautiful matchboard with sand, but the stains had worked their way into the heart of the wood.

Mama asked Papa, "Jack, isn't there some way we could do without Dan Singleton?"

"Aw, Carrie," Papa said, "his dad helped out here before you and I were born."

"I'm not talking about his dad," Mama said. "I'm talking about him."

Papa gave her a thoughtful look. He knew she was right, but he couldn't bring himself to dismiss Big Dan.

The following year, on Big Dan's first working day, Mama stopped him on his way in to breakfast.

"Mr. Singleton, there's to be no tobacco used in this house," she said. "If you must chew, go up behind the barn like the other men."

Big Dan turned on his heel, and to the other men he said, "You boys tell Jack Wister to git someone else to cut his damn corn!"

That was the last we saw of him.

When she heard about this, Mama said, "Well, I should hope so."

The next trip Papa made into the Gap, Big Dan met him at the iron bridge. Tildy gave him supper and a bed for the night.

"I hope you'll cut corn for us this fall, Dan," Papa said at supper.

Big Dan broke off a chunk of his wife's delicious cornbread. He swabbed it liberally in her special red-eye gravy, popped it into his mouth, and then washed it all down with buttermilk. "Things are too fancy at your place," he said. "Too damn many rules."

LEVI HARMAN

I used to wonder if there was a watch at the end of the gold chain that Levi Harman wore looped prominently across his middle. For some reason, I suspected there wasn't, but I admired him tremendously. It was 1903, and I was eight years old. When he came to our house "on business," as he said, he always addressed me as "Miss Nellie," as if I were grown up.

He wore a neat dark suit with a crisp, white shirt, a black string tie, and a black fedora. As he arrived at our gate, he took his hat off and struck it smartly with the edge of his flattened palm to shake the dust off. He then placed one foot after the other on the lowest rail of our whitewashed fence to brush off the dust.

The most memorable thing about him, however, at least from my point of view, was that he wore red socks. I never saw anyone else wear red socks. Moreover, he had a remarkable voice, resonant and almost bell-like. He made a point of addressing my father as "Jack."

Most men who came from places like Duncan's Creek, as he did, wanted to sell Papa something: a pig, a calf, or a pair of spring lambs. Or they wanted to borrow money. Mr. Harman, however, invariably opened his conversation by saying he was thinking of *buying* something from *us*.

"I hear you have some fine shoats this spring, Jack," he said. "I'm thinking of buying one for my brother Ike."

He sat on the front porch, his chair tipped back on its rockers, his boots propped on the railing. His pant legs were hitched up to show his red socks. In his resonant voice, he said, "I see by the papers, Jack, they're planning on laying a new railway bed in Tucker County. What's your opinion on that?"

"About time," Papa answered.

Mr. Levi said next, "I see, by the papers, the price of beef on the hoof is going up." After a moment, "I see, by the papers, there's going to be a new hotel in Keyser."

Our hired girl appeared in the doorway, clanging her bell for dinner. The big bell on the milk house roof rang. Down the road, Mrs. Flood's bell sounded. In the fields, the men laid down their tools.

Papa tipped his chair forward. "I hope you'll join us for dinner, Levi."

Mr. Harman followed Papa into the dining room, not the kitchen where the hired men sat. After eating, he accompanied Papa back to the porch.

"I'll think about those shoats of yours, Jack. By the way, I have a little mixed-breed heifer calf that might interest you."

He and Papa discussed its heredity and weight. Soon, Mr. Harman was on his way, with cash in his pocket and a promise to deliver the calf.

Sometimes Papa was not home when Mr. Harman came. I brought him a glass of buttermilk and a copy of the *Baltimore Sun*.

He said gallantly, "I do thank you, Miss Nellie."

Later, I found the paper neatly folded on the chair and the glass empty.

A few years later, Papa took me on a buggy ride to Duncan's Creek to pick up a girl who had agreed to work for us.

On a steep hillside above the creek we paused, and Papa pointed the buggy whip at two small cabins. "Levi Harman lives in that one," he said. "His brother Ike lives in the other." A slatternly woman emerged from the first cabin. Papa nodded to her. "That's his wife," he said.

By 1917, I was teaching school in Monroe County and was engaged to a man from there. The afternoon I arrived home with my fiancé, Edward, Mr. Harman happened to be sitting on the porch with Papa.

A streak of white in his hair, he stood up chivalrously for my introduction. "My, my, Miss Nellie," he said, "it surely is good to see you again." As Edward left the porch, Mr. Harman said in his wonderful voice, "I see, by the papers, Jack, there's talk of putting an iron bridge over Little Creek."

He had dinner with us and then sat for a time on the porch with Papa, Edward, and me.

When he left, Edward said, "Doesn't he have a horse?"

Papa shook his head.

Edward looked puzzled. "The way he talked, I figured he was some big shot."

Papa smiled. "Of course you did."

We watched Mr. Harman open the gate at the foot of the lawn, latch it behind himself, and walk down the road toward Duncan's Creek.

"He's just an old fellow who lives near here," said Papa.

"What's all that talk about what he reads in the paper?" Edward asked.

"Oh," Papa said, "he stops by the general store and listens to the talk. Then he comes here and tells it to us." Papa smiled. "He can't read."

"Can't *read*?" I interjected. "You never told me that."

Papa looked at Edward, then at me. "You never asked me."

A puff of dust hung over the roadstead where Mr. Harman had vanished. I was embarrassed, and sad, too, for my old friend.

"And to think I had him figured for some big shot," said Edward.

WILSE STRICKLAND

One day in 1904, Wilse Strickland came by our house. He was struggling to keep a two-handed grip on a snapping turtle's long, sharp, saw-toothed tail so its mean-looking snout couldn't bite him.

"I found him in your pond," he told my brothers and me. "So, by rights, he's yourn. Now, you-all put him in your swill tub and keep him there till he gets rid of the pond mud. Then he'll taste like chicken, some parts, and some parts will taste like pork tenderloin, and some parts will taste like beefsteak, and some like deer meat. Now you run and ask your mammy if she wants to keep him."

We sprinted off to the kitchen where Mama and our hired girl were sorting blackberries. Mama lifted her berry-stained hands from the pan and twisted around till she could see out the window. There stood Wilse, struggling with the turtle.

"Oh, why not," she said.

Wilse lugged the turtle around the milk house to the biggest swill tub, nudged the lid off, and swung the turtle up and over its rim. It disappeared with a splash; then its snout surfaced.

"Now then, you kids, besides your regular slops, dish-water, whey, and shelled corn, be sure to put in a little bran,"

Wilse said, "the way you do a hog before you butcher him. Be sure you tell Reuben." (He was our hired man.)

Wilse was on our land because he claimed the only boneset in Guthrie County grew in our calf lot and he had come to gather it. Boneset is a plant with fuzzy little grayish flowers. Old people in our part of West Virginia used it to set fractured bones. Mama used it to treat colds in the wintertime.

Wilse had a terrible laugh. He'd screw up his face, turn red, and begin to wheeze. And after a moment or two, he'd let out a sharp little bark *ha-ha*!

Once he picked his boneset, he sorted it into bunches, then hung them to dry in the milk house. "I picked enough for one and all!" he said, then laughed his terrible laugh. Later, he would came back to collect them.

"Why, Wilse, how nice," Mama always said. "That will come in handy this winter if the children have colds."

"Now then, missus," he said next, "I'll just sharpen your knives for you."

Sharpening our knives was his payment for the boneset. Out at the old storehouse, my brothers and I took turns cranking the handle of the big whetstone.

Word got out that we had a turtle in our swill tub. Children, from places like Duncan's Creek and up past the poor farm, came to see it.

"*We* wouldn't eat none of him," they said.

The novelty of the turtle wore off, and we were surprised when Wilse came back.

"Ask them women in your kitchen to give you kids some big pans," he told us.

He'd brought an ax and a long limber pole. He laid the pole across the rim of the tub. The turtle swam to the surface and snapped its jaws shut on the pole.

"He'll never turn loose of that till it thunders," Wilse told us.

My brothers and I helped Wilse lift the pole, with the turtle clamped onto it. We swung it out of the tub and onto the ground, ready for Wilse's ax.

Gazing down at the angry terrapin, Wilse hesitated, most likely thinking, *Wouldn't that snapper taste good on my table?*

"Gonna chop his head off, Missus Wister," he shouted toward the kitchen window.

"You do that, Wilse."

"You'll want to have a sharp knife ready, ma'am," he persisted, giving her one last opportunity to offer him the animal.

"I've cooked turtles, Wilse," Mama interrupted. "You just get its head off and be done with it."

Wilse's ax sailed high in an arc and hit its mark exactly. The turtle's head shot across the lawn, blood spurting from its neck.

"Turtles are like snakes," he told us as he pointed to its thrashing, headless body. "They don't die till the sun goes down."

We watched him cut away its shell. Blood splattered the early green apples that littered the wiry grass beside the milk house.

"Our old turtle's a she!" Wilse announced, pointing to a cluster of yellow yolks, which graduated from the size of a pea to Dayton's biggest aggie shooter.

All that remained of the turtle was its bloody shell and two huge pans of meat. Wiping his knife on the grass, Wilse asked, "Can you-all carry that one?"

We could. Grunting and pausing to switch our grips on the smaller of the two big graniteware pans, we set off across the yard. Wilse followed with the bigger pan.

"Turtle for your supper!" Wilse announced at the kitchen door. He set down his pan and then laughed his terrible laugh.

Mama cut the turtle into pieces and parboiled them as if they were parts of a tough, old laying hen. She then dried and rubbed them with salt, pepper, and flour. She set them in deep crocks in the milk house overnight. The next day, she fried them in butter and lard, and we had turtle for dinner.

"*Good*, Carrie," Papa said. "*Very good.*"

We all agreed.

I thought about all the trouble Wilse had gone to. He had traveled forty miles on horseback, from his home in Indian Spring, to butcher it. All of that, he said, was extra payment for the boneset.

Years later, Mama made me a "tight body," as we called it, a garment young girls wore in those days to confine their developing breasts. I had supposed that, in becoming a woman, I would put up my hair, let down my hems, and wear lisle stockings instead of the thick "ironclads" little girls wore.

One day, Mama was in the garden, and Reuben had taken my brothers to the mill. I was pleased to be alone in the kitchen. Something made me look up. In the doorway stood Wilse.

"I want Mr. Jack," he said, then turned around and left.

I had the impression he knew Papa wasn't home. I assumed he had come for his boneset.

I forgot about Wilse. The day was hot. I went to fetch a glass of cold buttermilk from the milk house, the same building where Wilse had hung the boneset to dry. As I turned to leave with my buttermilk, I found Wilse blocking my way. I had failed to hear him over the sound of the running water, which flowed through the cool building. He placed an arm across the passage.

Panicky, I called out, "Mama!"

Wilse flattened himself against the wall and let me pass.

Just then, Mama miraculously appeared on her way from the garden, holding a bouquet of parsley. She gave me a penetrating look and then turned to Wilse.

"Nellie, come in the house," she said.

In her room she said, "Does Wilse upset you, Nellie?"

I confessed that he did.

"We'll see he doesn't upset you again," she said.

I never saw Wilse after that.

I wonder if it was true, as he claimed, that we had the only boneset in Guthrie County. If so, I wonder if he ever found some in another county.

ROSCOE VANAMAN

If you believe a man lives on in the work he leaves behind, then Roscoe Vanaman continues to live on the farm where I grew up. He sold Mama the prune tree that still bears fruit behind the smokehouse. The snowball bush at our front gate was a bonus he awarded her for an order of apple trees. The bridal wreath on the opposite side of the gate was his bonus for pear trees she bought in 1904.

In April, he arrived, driving a pair of rangy, gray geldings and a market wagon groaning from its load of trees and bushes. Tied on behind was his suitcase for the fortnight he hoped to spend with us. Wearing a dark suit and black felt hat, he represented a nursery in Missouri. He lived nineteen miles from our farm, a distant world in those horse-and-buggy days.

On the day he arrived, the grass was turning green, but the March wind was still cold. My little brothers and I ran to tell Mama. She stuck her needle into the collar of her white shirtwaist. She folded her mending and laid it on top of her workbasket, then placed her thimble on top of that. She rose slowly and walked down the hall to the kitchen.

Mr. Vanaman was standing at the kitchen table, his catalogues spread across its oilcloth-covered surface. A sharpened lead pencil lay ready beside it. A flat wooden schoolroom pencil box held a fistful of extra pencils, also sharply pointed.

"My, my, Mrs. Wister," he said, "I see you've had a good winter! And how is Mr. Wister? And how are your mother and father?"

"They are well, thank you," Mama answered coolly. *Not so fast, please* was the message her tone implied. *We're not here to discuss my family.*

Mr. Vanaman's catalogue lay invitingly open to a picture of a pear tree. On the facing page was an illustration of a gleaming, dew-flecked pear. The tree was as round as a boxwood bush. Everyone knows pear trees are lanky and thin.

Mama sat down. Mr. Vanaman sat down.

"You once confessed to me you didn't own a single Kiefer pear!" he said.

While Mama and I studied his catalogue, he hitched his chair forward and then back. He crossed his legs and then uncrossed them. He pushed away from the table and then dragged himself back. He started up and then sank back, as if reminding himself, "Not yet!"

"Mr. Wister often stays in hotels, where I'm sure he's had a taste of the new Kiefer pears," he said. "I know he'll expect you to order a Kiefer pear." Mr. Vanaman looked at me. "I have a girl your age," he said. "She adores Kiefer pear butter and pickled Kiefer pears."

In his quick, nervous hand, he had already written Mama's order—four trees. He turned the page.

No matter how many trees Mama had ordered in the past, Mr. Vanaman could make her believe those varieties were inferior to the new kinds featured in his current book. He understood Mama. By nature, she was cautious and thrifty, but she was also fiercely competitive. He turned the page. A picture of another fat tree appeared, burdened with gleaming peaches.

"With the cost of peaches today, I advise you to plant a peach *orchard*," he said. "Men dote on peach pie, pickled

peaches, and brandied..." Remembering Papa was a teetotaler, he amended, "Spiced peaches."

Mama ordered a "peach orchard"—twenty trees.

Of Mr. Vanaman's apples, we had Paradise Sweet, Ben
Davis, Pearmain, Summer Rambo, and Early Harvest; of
plums, green gage, damson, and Stanley prune; and of cher-
ries, sour red, red sweet, Queen Anne, and Blackheart.

After writing Mama's order, he left the page unfin-
ished.

"I'll just drive down to Mrs. Flood's," he said.

Later, he came back for supper and to spend the night.
The next day, he was off again. After a week or two of these
daily jaunts, he hitched up his team, after first sitting down
with Mama to complete her order.

"We forgot raspberries," he said. "Cultivated raspberries are far superior to wild."

This wasn't true, but raspberries were Mama's favorite
fruit. In 1906, she ordered red, yellow, and black cultivate
varieties.

In his nervous way, Mr. Vanaman made his bonuses
seem like special gifts just *for us*, just *from him*. Beaming,
he said, "I'm giving you a nice, new double syringa, Mrs.
Wister. I want you to have this beautiful new pink rose.
When it blooms, I hope you'll think of me."

When the syringa first opened its small, fragrant, double, pure-white, waxy blooms and when those tiny roses,
like pink buttons, first appeared on the garden fence, we did
think of him. We could see him fidgeting with his freshly
sharpened pencils, crossing and recrossing his legs, and then
springing up to turn the page.

My brothers Dayton, left, and Hugh, right

AUTOMOBILES

One day, Sally Clayton called our farmhouse. She had been our switchboard operator for only a few months and could barely gasp out the words "An automobile is coming! A *real* automobile!"

"Slow down, Sally," Mama told her, stifling her own excitement.

"Central in Keyser says it just left there," Sally shrieked. "We expect it here tomorrow! Vestal will call me when it leaves there!"

Mama heard exclamations up and down the party line. Seven families were on the line. She hung up and sent my brother Dayton and me up the road to Mrs. Righter's to notify her about the automobile.

Mrs. Righter looked up from her well-worn Bible over the rims of her spectacles. *"What's the world coming to?"* she exclaimed.

Soon, Sally heard from Central in Vestal. The automobile would arrive there around noon and would reach us two hours later. It belonged to a Mr. Shank, Sally said. He owned the stagecoach franchise between Burlington and Keyser.

"Here it comes! Wait till you see it!" Sally hollered and broke off the connection.

We children flew down to the road and Mama followed, drawing a shawl around her shoulders. Our hired girls rang the dinner bell to notify the men in the fields.

Soon, we heard a dull throbbing like a threshing machine and saw a puff of dust in the distance. Before we could think, the wondrous machine was upon us.

It was black and had no roof. Two gentlemen in front wore dusters, goggles, visored caps, and gloves with gauntlets. In back, two ladies wore dusters and flowing chiffon veils. We had hardly taken all this in before the automobile vanished in clouds of dust.

Something lay on the road where it had passed! Dayton darted out and snatched it up—a red tam-o'-shanter!

Mama hung it on the coat tree inside the front door. "Whoever lost this will miss it," she said.

I thought, *Would someone write us a letter? Would they say, "To the owners of the white farmhouse set back among walnut trees: Did you find a red tam-o'-shanter?" Would the automobile come back? Would they give us a ride?*

Every man, woman, and child in Chinkapin Creek remembered the moment they'd seen the automobile. Our Uncle Vergil, capping hayshocks in his southwest field, heard the panting engine and saw the plumes of yellow dust rise off Amos Hill. As the automobile passed, he turned to his hired man and said, "I'm going to get me one of those things."

The next day, he came to Papa to borrow the money.

"Vergil," Papa said, "if I thought an automobile would help you make a living or be any good for this community, I'd say yes. But to sink three thousand dollars into a contraption like that—no."

Grandpa Cody, Uncle Vergil's own father, said, "That's too much money to throw away on a luxury, Vergil."

"There's a future in those contraptions, Pa," Uncle Vergil argued. "They won't *always* be just a luxury."

But Grandpa remained unmoved.

Two more automobiles came by that summer. Each time, Sally Clayton called us and each time, we children ran down to the road to watch it roar by.

"Don't call again, Sally." Mama said. "We've seen three automobiles! Nobody's paying us to look at automobiles. We have work to do."

One morning, a black automobile came chugging up our lane. The driver wore a duster, goggles, and gauntlets. On the high seat beside him sat a woman wearing a wide-brimmed hat swathed in veils. It was Uncle Vergil and his wife, Aunt Mary.

Uncle Vergil and his hired man Alf Hamrick had taken the stage to Keyser, spent the night at the Reynolds Hotel, picked up the automobile at the B&O freight yards, and driven to Vestal, where they spent another night, and the next day, they drove home to Chinkapin Creek.

Mama stared at her brother. "Where did you get the money, Vergil?"

"Mary's dad," Uncle Vergil said, and patted our aunt's arm.

Uncle Vergil's automobile was a Maxwell sports model, with a right-hand drive and room for two, including himself. To start it, he had to turn a crank between the front wheels.

Papa became even more opposed to automobiles after Uncle Vergil gave him a ride. "I'll never go near one of those things again!" he swore, knocking the dust from his coat and mopping his face with a handkerchief. "You should have seen Amos's horses! They kicked the bars off that big, new oak gate he built and took off straight for the river. Automobiles have no place on a working farm."

However, I noticed a copy of the *Baltimore Sun* open to an article about automobiles in the sitting room.

"Pent bought one," Papa said. Pent was his brother who lived in Martinsburg.

One morning, Papa looked down the table at Mama.

"I've been thinking, Carrie. The Ford Model T seems an economical family automobile."

Mama didn't look surprised.

How do you like it?" Papa asked Mamma two weeks later as Alf Hamrick drove our new Ford up to the kitchen gate. We could tell by his broad grin that despite whatever he had once thought of automobiles, he was proud to own one now.

"I'd like a ride in that, Mama said, and climbed into the rear seat.

Alf jammed a lever forward, and with a jolt, they were off.

From left, Alf Hamrick, Dayton, Papa, Mama

We housed our new automobile in the machine shed, alongside our sickle bar and manure spreader. The first time I heard the word "garage" was when Papa took me to Martinsburg to stay with Uncle Pent and Aunt Estie. They had just converted their carriage house and, like every family who had acquired an automobile, called it a "garage."

Automobile owners, discussing their garages, disagreed about how the word was pronounced. The Floods, who bought a Ford soon after we did, said "groog." Miss Annie Cutlip, my former grade school teacher, said the second syllable should rhyme with "lodge." Others claimed it should rhyme with "carriage."

Mama ordered a proper automobile-riding costume for herself—a duster of cream-colored linen and a long tobacco-brown veil of silk chiffon. She ordered a duster and veil of rich cream for me. Half a yard wide by two yards long and knotted becomingly under our ears, they streamed out behind us as we sailed along at twenty miles per hour. My little sisters, too young for veils, wore china-silk scarves—rose-colored for Bess and blue-green for Lily. Wearing our new finery, we piled in behind Alf Hamrick, borrowed once again from Uncle Vergil. Whenever poor Mr. Amos's horses heard us coming, they reared and snorted and bolted toward the river.

One day, as we rode, a familiar figure driving a team appeared, coming toward us on the narrow road.

Papa said, "Pull over, Alf. Stop till he gets by."

As the wagon passed, Ike Blizzard touched his hat. "That's all right, Mr. Wister. Doc and Star will just have to get used to these machines."

Our old buggy remained our chief means of transportation. Papa loved horses and was comfortable driving them. He never attempted to drive an automobile, but loved being driven. At twelve, I took over as driver, and soon after, my brothers Dayton and Hugh learned to chauffeur Papa as well.

Grandpa Cody bought a Buick. Mama's other brother bought a Model T Ford that had only one seat. Mr. John Morgan also bought a Ford. In time, everyone began to call their vehicles "cars."

All the same, some people resisted the new fad.

Mr. Will Cunningham said, "Julia and I aren't young anymore. We'll just stick to our old landau."

Mr. Amos Wister resented automobiles so bitterly that no one dared even mention them in his presence. Yet, one day, he accepted a ride from Papa. Thereafter, he never refused another ride. A small man in his fifties, Mr. Amos always sat in back wearing a pleased smile.

Horses, with the exception of Mr. Amos's, eventually got used to automobiles and only raised their heads briefly as they passed.

As for the red tam-o'-shanter, one day Papa gave it to Bess.

"I ran into Mr. Shank the other day," Papa told us. "He'd forgotten all about it."

"Was there a little girl in the car?" Bess asked. She loved the color red.

"Aw," Papa said, "I forgot to ask." From his pocket, he took out a blue tam-o'-shanter for Lily. He gave the rest of us presents of chocolate nonpareils and horehound sticks. By then, I was too old for any of this, or so I thought. Boys, of course, didn't wear tam-o'-shanters.

A new pastime—the Sunday drive—became popular. After church and midday dinner, families went motoring just for the fun of it. On one such outing, we drove to the remotest reaches of Guthrie County. I was at the wheel, with Papa at my side and Mama and my brothers in the back. A young girl appeared on her porch to watch us pass. She looked awed.

I remembered the morning not so long before when I'd seen *my* first automobile. But unlike the haughty Shank family in that first vehicle, I tried to convey, with a smile, *Don't let this car fool you. We're just folks like you.*

BEAN KIMBALL

B ean Kimball lived with his brother Noah in an old farmhouse not far from ours. "Noey," as everyone called him, was a justice of the peace and a well-respected citizen, but Bean was feeble-minded. He had a shock of yellow hair that hid his tiny blue eyes. In answer to whatever anyone said to him, he invariably said cheerfully, "Aw shucks."

One Snowy winter morning, the loafers hanging around Armistead's General Store were discussing a plan to send Bean calling on some of the local widows. They considered Mrs. Flood, who lived on the farm below ours; Mrs. Righter, half a mile in the other direction; Mrs. Ella Nash's shy, gentle daughter; and even Mrs. Lowry, our staid postmistress.

Mama's brother, Uncle Virgil, was a drinking buddy of Dr. John Hunter. He volunteered to bring the doctor's sleigh around. Uncle Virgil helped Bean up onto the driver's seat and handed him the reins.

"Now be sure to tuck Widow Flood in nice and warm," he told Bean. "Widows like little things like that."

He gave the mare a whack on the rump, and with a jingle of sleigh bells, Bean was off.

Maud Flood heard the sleigh arrive and ran out to meet it. "What do you *want*, Bean Kimball?" she demanded.

"I come to take the Widow Flood sleigh-riding," Bean said.

"Oh, go *on*, Bean!" Maud cried. "Ma don't want to go sleigh-riding with *you*. Ride on up the road and get Miss Carrie!" (She was my mother.)

At our stile, Bean slid down from his seat. He prized open the gate and plodded up to the house. I answered the door.

Mama had brought me up to be polite to everyone. "Bean," I said, "what brings you out on a day like this?"

"I come to take Miss Carrie sleigh-riding," Bean said.

Mama had known Bean all her life, and she knew how the local loafers treated him.

"We're just sitting down to dinner, Bean," she said. "Won't you join us?"

Bean said nothing. My brothers made room for him at the table. He ate well. Afterward, I helped him with his cap, scarf, and coat.

Back at Armistead's, Uncle Virgil said, "How did you and Widow Flood get along, Bean?"

"That Jack Wister, he's a good provider," Bean answered. "His wife, she sets a good table."

In time, Bean became known for saying, apropos of nothing anyone could identify, "That Jack Wister, he's a good provider. His wife, she sets a good table." The loafers who'd sent him on his errand forgot they'd done it. Bean's sandy hair turned white. Noey died. His daughter looked after Bean. On days when Bean turned up at the store, the latest generation of loafers hadn't the slightest idea what he was talking about.

JONATHAN MCCUE'S MISSUS

Across the river from Grandpa and Grandma Cody's farm there was a big old house like ours, with thick stone chimneys and double porches, set back from the road under old trees. It belonged to Grandma's cousin Polly McCue Kilgore. She lived there with her two bachelor brothers.

Cousin Polly was in her fifties and so was her brother Cousin Otis, but Cousin Jonathan was born half a generation later. In 1904, he was thirty-seven.

In those days, men cut their hair short, but Cousin Jonathan wore his long. He always dressed in a dark suit with a crisply pressed white-on-white shirt, a black string tie, and a sharply creased black fedora. He never did any work, just spent his days driving Cousin Polly's buggy slowly and sedately around the countryside. He sat reared back on the driver's seat with his shoulders very square and his black hair, with a streak of silver in it, curling like a drake's tail on his collar.

Grandma Cody, his first cousin, said, "Oh pooh! He ain't worth the powder it would take to blow him up!" He had tried to court girls in her day, but no one would have him.

One morning, our postmistress was sitting in her little front room, which she never used for government business, sewing herself an apron. Cousin Polly's buggy drew up in

41

front, with Jonathan in the driver's seat. She set her workbasket aside and went to the door.

"Mr. McCue, what brings you here this nice morning?"

He swept off his fedora, bowed deeply, and said in his resonant voice, like that of a state senator, "I'm waiting on the stage, Mrs. Lowery. I've come to meet my missus."

Although Cousin Jonathan's faults were many, no one had ever called him a liar. Mrs. Lowery hurried back insidedoors to tell her daughter, who was hemstitching pillowslips for her hope chest.

Miss Belle looked out the window. Across the road, Miss Bea Nelson and *her* daughter were making pear butter from the fruit of a little Seckel pear tree that grew in their yard. They came out to stare. Miss Belle joined them to report that Jonathan McCue was there in his sister's buggy waiting for his missus to arrive.

"Belle Lowery, you show me a bag of gold dollars in the chimney place," Miss Bea said, "then I'll believe you."

At that moment, a puff of dust appeared in the distance. The stage was on its way.

Mr. Reddle, the stage driver, who had never helped anybody in or out of his vehicle, stepped down and offered his hand to a lady. Wearing a braid-and-feather hat and carrying a black alligator-cloth Boston bag, she looked very sure of herself.

"You must be Mrs. Simmons," Cousin Jonathan said in his resonant voice. "I'm Mr. McCue."

The loafers, who'd been sitting in Armistead's store, came to the porch to stare. Miss Nettie Hunter appeared on her portico with a hairbrush. They all watched Mr. Reddle unstrap Mrs. Simmon's grips and set them on the ground beside the stage.

Cousin Jonathan introduced everyone to his missus.

Miss Nettie couldn't be counted on to answer because she took laudanum. Everyone else said they were glad to meet Mrs. Simmons.

"Well?" Mrs. Lowery whispered, crooking a finger at Mr. Reddle.

"I picked her up in front of Pickering's Hotel in Record," Mr. Reddle whispered back. "She got off the stage there from Baltimore. She's a widow and has a private income. She put an advertisement for a husband in the *Baltimore Sun* and got over a hundred answers. His was the best."

"Well, I never!" Mrs. Lowery exclaimed.

Cousin Jonathan handed his missus into the buggy, climbed up beside her, and touched his whip to the horse. The stage, empty after Mrs. Lowery took the mail sack, set off toward Minerva.

Everyone related to that branch of the McCues, which included Mama, attended the party Cousin Polly gave for Cousin Jonathan's missus. The guest of honor impressed everybody when, with a bunch of wheat straws taken out of her alligator-cloth bag, she quickly constructed a tiny house, complete with a window, door, chimney, and a wee porch. She made a hit with Cousin Polly when she presented it to her.

Cousin Jonathan acted as if he never expected anything else in a bride. "She plays the organ," he said. "She sings. She does embroidery." He passed around a silk handkerchief with "JMcC" embroidered in purple floss on the corner. "She cooks. She made the brownstone cake you're about to eat. She fried the chicken. She made the slaw."

Mrs. Lowry whispered to Mama, "She dyes her hair."

"Hush, Bea," Mama whispered back. "Jonathan McCue is a *very* lucky man."

Cousin Jonathan's missus made a wheat-straw house for everybody who'd been at Cousin Polly's dinner. Mama's small house sat in a place of honor on our kitchen windowsill for as long as I can remember. Mrs. Flood hung hers over her dining room table, where it turned dark and furred over with dust. As for Cousin Jonathan, he never did any more work than he ever had, but because of his missus, his stock went up everywhere. Cousin Polly gave him a corner of her farm, where he and his missus put up a nice brick house with three porches. He got invited places he'd never even heard of, and everybody said there had to be *some* good in a man who could get a lady like that to marry him.

Max Hamrick

There was a side of farm life my mother hid from my sisters and me, though our brothers knew all about it. Mama referred to this as "men's work."

One day, Ernest Tolley told me that Papa and his father were working on "cut calves." I asked Mama what Ernest meant by "cut calves." With a startled look, she said that a young man should not talk of such things in the presence of a young lady. Ernest was my age, eleven, and I had a crush on him. But I was shocked at his indiscretion and never felt the same about him again.

I couldn't help but think that "cut calves" had something to do with Dr. Jared Dickerson, a veterinarian, who made annual springtime visits to our farm. Wearing heavy coveralls, he worked for two or three days in the log stable and the stoutly fenced-in lot behind it.

I once dared to ask Mama what Dr. Dickerson did there. She studied me for some time, then said, "Men's work," and changed the subject.

Dr. Dickerson smelled of disinfectant. His bedroom also smelled of disinfectant, as did the hallway outside. For weeks after he left, that part of the house reeked of it.

Our neighbor Royce Flood owned a big sorrel traveling horse. When Royce brought his horse to the stable, Mama kept us girls busy in the kitchen. Our hired man Reuben took Nan, our stocky, little gray saddle mare, to the stable and closed the doors.

Maud Flood, Royce's half sister, said, "Nellie, you know what they're doing in there, don't you?"

"I assume they're shoeing the horses," I said.

One day, in the schoolyard, Maud said, "Look at Verdie Harman's stomach, Nellie." For the first time, I noticed that it was oddly larger. When I asked Maud why, she smiled, but didn't answer. Verdie and Mr. Joe Waggoner ran away to Cumberland, Maryland. They came back married. I wondered about the baby boy they brought back with them, but I drew no conclusions.

Maud seemed to know things she shouldn't. I envied her knowledge, but I also felt superior. Her mother was wrong to let her know these things. Mama said so. That's why, though Maud and I were close friends, Mama never let me go home from school or spend the night with her.

Iva Finch was another classmate who knew things she shouldn't. She was the daughter of our hired man Paris Finch and his wife, Dovey. Iva plaited her hair into one long heavy braid and liked to toss it about. "You don't know *anything*, Nellie Wister," she'd tell me, swinging her braid defiantly. But when Iva tried to tell me her secrets, I turned away. In my opinion, she was a common girl because she knew such things. I would grow up to be a "lady" because I did not.

Still, I wondered what Iva and Maud knew. I thought about Annie Laurie Slattery and Em and Gertie Finch, who had children but no husbands. Mama said these women were "loose." I didn't know what she meant, but trusted that she would tell me when she was ready.

Every summer or so, Max Hamrick came to stay with us for a few days and brought along a very high-spirited stallion.

Mama disliked Max. He had no skill with people, she said, and even less with animals. One day, Mate and Kate, Mama's favorite pair of draft mares, was taken to the stable along with Max's stallion, which Max seemed barely able to control.

Mate and Kate were everybody's favorites. They had wonderful dispositions, yet were so powerful they could plow twelve acres without apparently noticing they had done it. Mama watched Reuben lead the mares to the barn. Max fought to control his stallion, for the big stud's attention was fixed on the mares. Max's angry outbursts only enraged the stallion. Mama wiped her hands nervously on her apron, shook her head, and went inside.

Half an hour passed. Then, from behind the barn, we heard Papa's voice rise as we had never heard it. Profane outbursts came from Max and a shrieking of horses, followed by Papa's furious shout, "Stop him, Max! Stop it! Get him off her! Get him out of here!"

Mama ushered us children into the sitting room and closed the door. Even so, we could hear the commotion, which continued for some time. Mama's face was white. From the barn, Max appeared riding his stallion. Doubled over in pain, clutching his side, he was barely able to stay in the saddle. Blood poured from his head and shoulders. At the foot of the lane, he turned toward the town of Minerva.

Papa appeared from the barn, trembling with rage—a rare emotion for him. At dinner, he picked distractedly at his food and then left the table. A pall had fallen over us. After dinner, we cleaned up in silence.

Mrs. Pennybacker sent me out to the milk house for milk and butter. As I crossed the lower porch, I glanced toward the calf lot. Kate lay there, motionless. Mate stood beside her, nudging her, as if to rouse her. I brought the milk and butter and then went back for cream. Mate was still trying to urge her up. After a while, Mate moved off down the lot. Kate hadn't moved, just lay stretched out with her head facing away.

Back in the kitchen, I reported what I had seen. Mrs. Pennybacker wiped her hands on her apron and followed me outside. She glanced briefly at the calf lot. Without saying a word, she went to find Mama. After speaking with Mama, she set off toward the barn to look for Reuben.

I knew that Kate would never get up and that whatever had happened to her had something to do with Max Hamrick and his stallion.

Mama looked stricken. She gathered us children into her room, told us to stay there, and shut the door.

I knew I shouldn't, but I slipped out of the room, down the hall, outside, and across the field.

Mate had returned and was again nudging Kate. She looked to me as if to say, *Here's Nellie. She'll help.*

I touched Kate. She felt warm, but she was dead. I didn't want to cry in front of Mate; I wanted to comfort her.

Papa had Kate's body dragged three miles up over the mountain behind our house. Every evening, when the wind changed direction, we smelled her and saw buzzards circling. In time, the smell faded.

Several weeks later, Max Hamrick's badly bruised body was discovered floating in Chinkapin Creek, caught in the roots of a willow tree. His magnificent stallion was found grazing a few miles below the village.

Had the stallion turned on him? Had the stallion attacked Kate?

Neither Papa nor Mama would ever say what had happened that day.

Maud Flood #3, and Nellie Wister #1

MILLIE FLOOD

One day Mama said "I believe Millie Flood would have been a different person if she'd been allowed to see people."

"Well," Papa said, "I guess Edgar's folks did what they thought was right at the time."

They went on to talk about other things. It was 1906, and I was eleven.

I'm sure there were people in our community who had no idea Millie existed. She must have been Mama's age—twenty-nine or so. She had clear, smooth skin, pretty brown eyes, glossy brown hair, and small hands and feet. But she couldn't talk. I mean, she wasn't *able* to talk. Her mouth hung open, as if she were on the verge of saying, "Oh," but no word came out. What ailed her was a birth defect that affected the roof of her mouth. She could not breathe normally.

Millie lived with the widow of her brother Mr. Edgar Flood. In large families, in those days, an overlapping of generations was common. Older children married and began having babies while their mothers gave birth to their last children.

Millie was allowed into only two parts of the big farmhouse. She shared the bedroom with a woman they called "Aunt Betty." Sometimes, if no one was around, she went into the kitchen. Aunt Betty had gray hair and very small features. I doubt she was a real aunt, probably just one of those women farm families sometimes had living with them because of distant kinship or widowhood. She was the only person in the Flood household who was kind to Millie.

"Oh, Millie," the Flood children said, "get out of the way! Nobody wants to see *you*!" I could never have said such a thing to an adult.

Mrs. Flood herself said, "Oh, *hush*, Millie!"

Some days when I went to Floods' to play with my friend Maud, I found Millie and Aunt Betty in the kitchen. Aunt Betty sat in the sheepskin-covered rocking chair carding wool or cutting up rags to make into rugs. Close by her, Millie moved continuously, taking one step forward, then a step back, not achieving anything in particular. I never saw either of them go into any other part of the house. The Floods didn't want people to know Millie existed.

When I came in, Millie sometimes made a hollow sound, something like blowing air across the neck of a bottle. If Maud was there, she'd exclaim, "Oh, *shut up*, Millie! Nellie hasn't come here to see *you*!" Millie would turn away and not look at me.

One day, without giving it much thought, I answered the funny noises Millie made. I said, "I'm fine, Millie, how are you?"

I was surprised at myself. *Had I really understood her?*

No one else was present. Millie repeated her usual sounds, but held the syllables longer and gave them an emphasis I'd never heard: *haangh* haangh *haangh* haangh haangh haangh *haangh*.

What did that mean?

After that, each time I went to the Floods', if no one else was around, Millie uttered the same succession of sounds, some of which were emphasized. One day, it came to me what she meant: "How are all of them at home?"

"Everyone at home is fine, Millie," I told her.

After that, whenever I went to the Floods' and found her alone, she greeted me.

"*Haangh* haangh *haangh* haangh haangh haangh *haangh?*"

I answered that we were fine.

One day, Millie said something new. I seemed to be able to decipher it: "How's your Mama?"

"Mama's making quince jelly," I said.

"I like quince jelly," Millie said. I mean, I *knew* that was what she said.

I told Mama about this. She said, "Next time you go to the Floods', take Millie a jar of quince jelly."

As I handed Mama's present to Millie, Maud grabbed it away. "That's not for *you*, Millie!" she said.

"Maud, Mama sent it to Millie," I said.

"Oh, *what next?*" Maud exclaimed, and slammed the jar down hard.

"*Hanh* hanh *hanh*-hanh hanh *hanh*," Millie said. "Thank your mama for me."

After that, Millie became a different, less mysterious person to me.

How could I understand her?

Her pretty brown eyes looked directly into mine. She said, "How is your Papa? And how's your new baby sister?"

One day, I arrived at the Floods' to find the house empty.

"Maud?" I called. "Aunt Betty? Mrs. Flood? Charley? Joe?"

There was no answer.

Then I remembered that Maud's brother Joe was driving them across the mountain to the dentist in Harrisonburg.

I found Millie and Aunt Betty on the front porch. Aunt Betty relaxed in a rocking chair, and Millie perched on a bench beside her. As I opened the screen door, Millie gave me a welcoming smile.

"*Haangh* haangh *haangh* haangh haangh haangh *haangh*?" she said. "How is everyone up at home?"

I gave her my usual reply.

"Haangh haangh *haangh* haangh haangh?" she then asked. "It's a nice day, ain't it?"

I heard something new in her voice. She could go outside the house if she wanted to. Anyone could drive by and see her there. There she was.

The Flood family came home. Without saying a word, Mrs. Flood hurried up the steps. Charlie and Joe followed and disappeared into the house.

"Well, *what next?*" Maud exclaimed as she caught sight of Millie on the porch. "Millie! Get inside before someone sees you!"

Millie complied.

I never again saw Millie on the porch. The Floods never stopped saying, "Oh, shut up, Millie! No one wants to see *you*."

Millie, however, stopped her restless pacing. She sat calmly at Aunt Betty's side, helping her card wool and cut up rags to weave into carpeting. Every time she saw me, she asked how Mama and Papa and everyone was at home.

Miss Lou and Charley Wister

MISS LOU

My father worked half the year as collector of internal revenue for the six counties in West Virginia's eastern panhandle. In the late fall, he traveled the hundred and twenty miles from his office in Martinsburg to our farm to be home for hog butchering. One November night in 1906, he stood warming his coattails by the sitting room fire when a knock came at the door. There stood his cousin Charley Wister.

In those days, our county roads were single lane and unpaved, for horse or foot travel. No one traveled at night.

Charley had consumption, what we now call tuberculosis. It was incurable. Every fall, Charley traveled to Arizona for the dry climate. He rode horseback sixty miles from his farm to ours, rested a few days with us, and then boarded the stagecoach for the seventy-mile trip to Keyser. From there, he took the train. The following April or May, he returned by the same route.

Charley was a big man. Papa lifted the lamp so it shone into his gray eyes. They were bright with fever.

"I...always...catch...a little...something...coming...across... North...Mountain...", Charley said.

Papa turned to Mama, "Carrie, have the bed changed in my room."

"Papa's room," where he worked when he was home, was upstairs. In cold weather, my brothers slept there, for it was warm. That night, Papa had built a fire in its small sheet-iron stove.

Mama had been reading *Pilgrim's Progress* to us children. She slipped the horn pins from her hair, which hung gleaming to her waist. "Dayton, go with your papa," she told my brother. "See what he needs." She turned to me. "Nellie, go wake Mrs. Pennybacker. Tell her to change the bed in Papa's room. *Hurry*!"

Dayton scooted up the front stairs. I ran the other way, out through the darkened house to the kitchen and then up the back staircase. I passed the hired-men's room, with its exciting aroma of sweat and plug tobacco, on my way to the housekeeper's room.

Mrs. Pennybacker wriggled out of her flannel nightgown and into a blue wash dress. She knotted the strings of an apron, took up the lamp, and followed me down the narrow back stairs. Our shadows leapt along its walls.

"Bring sheets and pillowslips, Nellie," she told me. "Bring flannel rags from your mama's basket and as many hot bricks as you can carry."

In cold weather, we heated bricks on the sitting room hearth to warm our beds.

In the sheepskin-covered rocker in Papa's room, Charley sat close to the stove. His heavy overcoat was draped around his shoulders, and Grandma Wister's piecework comforter swaddled his knees. Mrs. Pennybacker and I wrapped hot bricks in wool flannel and slid them between the sheets of the big walnut bed. Dayton opened the little stove's mica-paned door and pitched in corncobs to make the fire burn hot.

Sometimes my brothers debated who would inherit Papa's watch. "I'm the oldest," Dayton said. Hugh held his tongue. Charley's watch, which lay on top of Papa's desk, was of heavy dark-yellow gold. Its lid was lined with a silk disk, on which were painted tiny figures of ladies in hoop skirts and gentlemen in velvet waistcoats. My brothers' eyes were fixed on Charley's watch.

Mrs. Pennybacker slipped the last hot flannel-wrapped brick between the sheets. We heard Papa's voice on the telephone downstairs: "Lou, you better come."

Who was Lou?

"The room's ready," Mrs. Pennybacker said. "Go tell your Papa."

The odor of horse sweat, mixed with the scent of burning logs, filled the warm sitting room. Papa had just taken care of Charley's horse.

Mama looked at me. "Nellie, in the morning, you and Dayton go down to the gate and help Miss Lou with her grips." In the lamplight, her eyes looked enormous.

Miss Lou...? I thought. *Her grips...?*

"We all must be extra kind to Miss Lou," Mama added.

The stagecoach driver usually allowed his passengers to unstrap their own grips and boxes. He often flicked his reins before they had time to get out of his way. Dayton and I were amazed when he eased himself down and offered his hand to a tall red-haired lady.

"Good-bye, Miss," he said in a raspy voice we'd never heard. "Good luck."

Miss Lou wore a blue coat, a blue sailor hat, and a brooch in the shape of a pair of linked gold hearts. Coppery hair sprang out around her freckled forehead. Our gate's ploughshare weight clanged shut behind her. She directed at us a startled, unseeing stare, which seemed to say, *Where am I? And who are you?*

Dayton and I wrestled her grips into the wheelbarrow and trundled it squeaking over the frozen grass. Our little sister, Bess, followed us. On the porch, Mama hugged a shawl around her shoulders.

"I *told* him to leave before it got so cold!" Miss Lou burst out in a raspy voice as odd as her appearance. "I *told* him!"

Mama shot her a warning look: *Not in front of the children.* She and Mama hurried into the house. Dayton and I ran around the other way to the kitchen. Ola Smith, Mrs. Pennybacker's young helper, was washing the breakfast dishes.

"She thinks he's a-going to marry her," Ola said. "She has another thing a-coming."

"What are you telling these children?" Mrs. Pennybacker demanded. "Miss Lou is here to take care of him. He's going to get better."

Bess had caught up to us. Her eyes shone like pawpaw seeds.

"What will happen to his watch?" Dayton broke in.

"His boy will get his watch," Ola said. "A boy always gets his daddy's watch."

"Ola, it's time to boil the crock lids," Mrs. Pennybacker said.

Mama gave Miss Lou the room Bess and I slept in. She moved Dayton and Hugh into a bedroom off the back hall. Before breakfast, we children crept down the back stairs. Miss Lou wore a pink apron over a blue wash dress. She was lugging basins, slop jars, and trays up to Charley, amid the resinous, licorice-sweet scent of balm of Gilead. Another odor, equally strange in our house, marked the liquor-soaked presence of Dr. Sam Hunter.

It was wash day. Ginny Hamrick had hiked the two miles from her house to ours. The powerful, sharp-smelling steam of homemade soft soap poured from the washhouse chimney. By noon, the clothesline between the washhouse and the garden fence creaked with the weight of sheets flapping in the wind. The kitchen reeked of the metallic odor of sad irons heating on the big wood-burning range. There were also the fumes of another of Miss Lou's concoctions, some kind of tar-and-vinegar mixture. Charley's hacking cough echoed through the house.

At breakfast, Miss Lou's hair sprang like copper filings from its pins. A skipped buttonhole showed a loop of pink ribbon over her full bosom. Papa rolled up his napkin sooner than usual and left the table. Having Miss Lou around was hard for him in a house like ours, where Mama saw to it that no small thing was ever out of place. Ola, carrying fresh biscuits from the kitchen, whispered, "Your daddy ought to throw out a woman as sloomy as that!"

A snapshot in Mama's album shows Charley sitting in Papa's oak swivel chair, out on the upstairs porch. Charley's handsome face looks flushed. His dark fedora hat lies on the porch wood box. Miss Lou stands behind him. Her tremendous energy doesn't show in the print, nor does his fever. Looking at this picture, one might ask, *Why is that big man wrapped up like that, and why does that pretty woman look so miserable?*

Charley's lungs rasped like a rotten old leather bellows. "This...is...a... pretty...pass...Barbara Ann..." he said.

"I'm *Nellie*," I said. "I'm *Nellie*, Cousin Charley."

Miss Lou bustled in.

"Who's Barbara Ann?" I asked her.

"Did he ask for her?" her voice broke. "She's dead." In a near whisper, she said, "She was his wife."

I awoke to the cranking of the wall telephone downstairs.

"Tall, Matt," Papa said. "A tall man."

Beside me, Bess breathed noisily in her sleep.

"Matt" was Mr. Waybright, whose carpentry shop displayed coffins. His wife lined them with shirred peach-colored or pale-blue silk.

Mrs. Pennybacker rolled out biscuit dough. Ola used Grandma Wister's ham knife to slice side meat. A snuff stick tucked under her lower lip, Ginny Hamrick sat in the chimney corner. Our cows bawled, and the hired men called them, "Hooey! Hooo-eeee!"

Ola swept ham, the color of whet leather, into the big iron skillet and shoved it ringing onto a stove eye. "I wouldn't be in her shoes for all the money in Guthrie County!" she muttered.

I wondered how I would feel if I were an old maid, alone and far from home, with so much life in me that it flew off like sparks.

The little stove in Papa's room had been allowed to go out. The scent of camphor and carbolic acid tainted the cold air. Charley lay on the bed, wearing the brown suit he'd traveled in. His shapely, long-fingered hands lay folded on his chest. I'd seen three other dead people: Grandpa and Grandma Wister and Dr. Sam Hunter's baby girl. How dark their faces looked, like used-up sassafras root!

"He wanted me to have it!" Miss Lou cried suddenly.

"If it's in his will, you can," Papa said. "But, for now, hand it over."

Papa and Miss Lou stood at the far end of the room. She swung a hand forward, and something flew through the air. As Papa caught it, openhanded, she dashed out of the room.

Miss Lou had flung something else at Papa. It was her heart-shaped brooch. Through his fingers spilled the chain of Charley's gold watch.

Within moments, Miss Lou came storming back, one arm shoved through the sleeve of her blue coat, the other hand clamping her blue sailor hat to the side of her head. She kicked her grips along the hallway, then *Bump! Crackety bang! Thump!* down the stairs. The lace edge of a peach-colored petticoat protruded from one case. Embarrassed for her, I nudged the case around to hide the offending sight. I wished that Papa would make an exception about Charley's watch.

Charley's son and an older man sat at the breakfast table gobbling down a meal of cold ham, buttered light bread, and smearcase. Wheatley had his father's handsome long-jawed face and gray eyes, and his voice was so much like Charley's that it startled me.

He said, "Cousin Carrie, we couldn't *make* him leave earlier. None of us could've done a thing."

Wheatley and his neighbor had driven a spring wagon, a common farm vehicle in those days, sixty miles over winter roads. They were planning on traveling straight back. Our hired men had saddled Charley's big bay and strapped on his saddle pockets. In our buggy sat Papa, swaddled in a buffalo robe. He had another buffalo robe for Miss Lou and extra charcoal foot warmers for their feet. Mama stood wrapped in her shawl by the back fence.

Where was Miss Lou?

"There she is!" Hugh shouted. She sat on the bare bed of the spring wagon. Her feet were thrust out straight, and an arm lay across Charley's coffin.

"Lou, dear," Mama pleaded, "ride in the buggy with Jack."

"I don't hold anything against *you*, Carrie," Miss Lou said. Papa flapped his reins, and the buggy jolted into motion. The spring wagon followed. Wheatley, on his father's bay, brought up the rear.

The day Papa came home, the ruts in our farm lanes were no longer frozen, but glistened with mud. Snowflakes the size of goose down floated around.

"Charley left Lou five hundred dollars," Papa told Mama.

Five hundred dollars was a fortune in those days, but Mama frowned. "What will become of her, Jack?"

"Wheatley's a level-headed fellow," Papa said. "He'll do the right thing. She'll go on living there at the spring."

But people would talk. They'd remember how Miss Lou carried on in the wagon. No one would want her after that.

In 1911, Papa and I rode across North Mountain. It was the same road, winding and steep, that Charley had traveled four years before, the same road along which Papa, Wheatley, and his neighbor had carried Charley's body, and Miss Lou with it, home.

At fifteen, I was excited to be making the trip. The rose-pink azalea we called "honeysuckle" filled the air with its spicy fragrance. Hawks wheeled above the ridges. Papa had kept his family's property at Indian Spring. Our tenant occupied a log house hung with bear and wildcat skins. His wife gave us a supper of home-cured ham and fried hominy. Papa and I inspected our latest crop of calves and colts and some cows recovering from having eaten laurel during the spring drive. We looked at timber ready to be cut. Papa showed me the log house where he was born. It had become a dilapidated ruin, tangled over with pink rambler rose. We rode on to have dinner at a nice-looking farmhouse.

I had no trouble recognizing the man who welcomed us. Charley's calm, level eyes looked out of his son's handsome face.

"Wheatley and Miss Lou are married, Nellie," Papa told me.

I remembered Mama's remark: "Charley is older than she is by twelve years." So Wheatley and Miss Lou, I reasoned, were about the same age.

The house had the same double chimneys and double porches as ours. It had the same separate kitchen as our house once had. Like ours, it was weather-boarded over and painted white. Only people who grew up in such houses would know that its core was of logs.

Miss Lou showed me a counterpane that had been her mother's and a dresser of butternut wood made by someone in Wheatley's family. On top of the dresser lay the gold brooch she had thrown at Papa.

From her apron pocket, she produced Charley's big, beautiful gold watch. She opened it with a well-practiced flip of the thumb. "Look at the time, Nellie!" she said. "You're staying for dinner, of course."

In her coppery eyes was the most serene expression I have ever seen.

GEORGE RENFREW

(A PLACE TO REST)

One July morning in 1907 Mr. Harold Smith came hotfooting it down the road to our farm. He was out of breath and plainly upset.

"Mr. Wister! Mr. Wister!" he gasped, so winded he could hardly form the words. "I think you better come!"

The day was blistering hot. Papa had just come from a cattle-buying trip, and wanted to get out of his traveling clothes and into something fresh. He wanted to sit in the shade on the front porch and gather his wits. Instead, he followed Mr. Smith up the dusty road to the county poor farm. Among other things, Papa was county commissioner for the poor.

Harold Smith was the poor farm's hired superintendant. He was a calm, efficient man a decade or so younger than Papa, who was fifty-one. Papa valued his sense of humor and often confided in him.

What emergency could have so upset him?

Papa knocked at the door of one of the small cabins that housed the poor farm's inmates, the ones who could be counted on to look after themselves, to some degree at least. He heard the scrape of a chair, then hesitant footsteps. A small, emaciated man opened the door. He wore rags, but looked clean. His age was hard to guess—forty, fifty, or even much older, Papa thought.

"This is Mr. Renfrew," Harold Smith said. To the stranger he said, "Mr. Wister here is our county commissioner for the poor."

Papa thought Mr. Renfrew's clothing might once have been expensive. The soles of his shoes had almost totally separated from the uppers; they were held together by bits of string.

In an educated accent, the stranger said, "Mr. Wister, I need a place to rest."

"This is our county farm," Papa said. "It's where we house our poor who can't look after themselves. Some of them are feeble-minded. You don't want to stay here."

He wondered how Mr. Renfrew had managed to wander into our valley. Judging by his speech, he wasn't from West Virginia, or even Virginia or Maryland. Papa thought he might be from a place like New York.

"Come on home with me," he said. Then it occurred to him that Mr. Renfrew might have something contagious. He turned to Mr. Smith. "He can stay here for the time being." Once outside the cabin, he said, "See that he's comfortable, Harold. Have his food brought to him."

"At least the cabin's single," Harold Smith said. "I'd hate to see him share a room with Joey-Bird Carson or Dave Sowers."

Joey-Bird Carson and Dave Somers were permanent residents of the poor farm. Joey-Bird had a bullet-shaped head, crossed eyes, and the mind of a two-year-old. Dave Sowers often ran away to beg for pennies. If you offered him any coin except a penny, he'd fly into a rage. "Gonna sue you! Gonna sue you!" he'd shout. He had no idea what the words meant.

Mr. Renfrew's cabin, about six by eleven feet, contained a bed, a table and chair, a wood stove, and a wood box. It had a single small window, a coal-oil lantern, and nails to hang clothes on.

The following day, when Papa checked on Mr. Renfrew, he found him reading a book. The volume was thin, its pages badly stained. The frail little man had carried it on what must have been a very long journey. Papa was startled when he saw the book's title—*The Death of Ivan Ilych*.

"Would you like to read it?" Mr. Renfrew asked.

"I would," Papa answered. That night, he read Tolstoy's story about a man who learns he is dying and realizes he has lived a fruitless life. He married a vain, superficial woman, his children are strangers, he has reached middle age with only material possessions to show for himself, and he dies a slow, painful death.

Papa sat staring at the book. He had married for love. He had prospered. He made a point of knowing each of his children individually. A religious man, he strove to give worldly things no more than their due. He was healthy. Yet, what if he should learn he had only months to live?

The sky grew light, and the wheat fields turned a rich gold. With a kind of wonder, Papa thought about his own good fortune. He thought about the sick man up the road.

The next day, he found Mr. Renfrew's cabin empty. Howard Smith's wife appeared at the springhouse door. She pointed toward the mountain. Papa saw the county's newest ward, wearing a pauper's blue shirt and overalls, sitting under a red cedar tree. He turned his horse in that direction.

"This is the best place," said Mr. Renfrew, in greeting.

Papa stared at him. He found it hard to admire a place where his county's most pathetic citizens were buried. On the ground beside Mr. Renfrew, a small forked branch held a thimble-sized nest—a humming bird's, Papa thought.

"I never paid attention to things like this," the sick man said.

A haze hung over the field where Harold Smith's men were cutting wheat. Across the valley, the river sparkled in the sun. Beyond the river rose a long line of blue hills.

"After the leaves are off the trees," Papa said, "you might walk up to the ridge there. Hazelnuts ripen up there in October."

"I'll be here," Mr. Renfrew said. Something in his tone made Papa's heart sink.

The next day one, of the poor farm's inmates shut a gate on his hand. Mr. Renfrew ordered him to be brought into the infirmary. He skillfully dressed, splinted, and bandaged the man's hand and prescribed medication.

Harold Smith said, " I'll lay you he's a doctor and knows what's wrong with him."

At the next session of the county court, Papa argued that Mr. Renfrew be allowed to stay on at the poor farm.

"I don't know who he is or where he's from," Papa said. "If it costs the county money, I'll pay. He won't be here long."

Our community doctor was far gone in drink, and Papa had decided that, in any case, his services wouldn't be necessary.

The next time he checked, he found Mr. Renfrew folding a sheet of paper into an envelope.

"Don't open it now," he said. "You've been more than kind to me. I only wish you and I had met under other circumstances."

Papa thought it unlikely Mr. Renfrew would live another month. He wasn't surprised when, soon after, Harold Smith sent for him. Mr. Renfrew was dead.

In Mr. Renfrew's envelope was a sheet of cheap note-paper on which he had expressed his gratitude to Guthrie County and to Papa personally. He'd requested that, if the court would allow it, he be buried in the paupers' graveyard. At the bottom of the sheet, he added, as if as an afterthought, a telephone number in Massachusetts.

Papa wondered who or what was in Massachusetts.

A woman answered his call. "I know a George Renfrew," she said.

Papa explained the reason for his call and asked if she would be coming to West Virginia. A silence ensued, and continued. Papa believed something had happened to the connection, a common occurrence in those days.

He was about to hang up when the woman abruptly said, "No," and hung up.

Papa chose a spot under the big red cedar outside the paupers' graveyard for Mr. Renfrew's grave. As the coffin disappeared into the earth, the scent of oak tannin drifted coolly down the mountain. Papa heard the sick man's frail voice: *This is the best place.*

In October, a large black automobile appeared in our lane and stopped at the front gate. It's uniformed driver came to the door and asked for Mr. Wister. Our hired girl Ola went to fetch Papa. As he went to meet the automobile, a small woman emerged. He supposed she might be forty years old or perhaps younger. She wore a blue tailored suit and matching hat.

"I'm Helen Renfrew," she said. "George Renfrew was my husband."

Something about her put Papa off.

"I expect you've come for his things," he said. "There isn't much. Let me show you his grave."

At the poor farm, men were raking up corn stubble. As the black automobile passed the institution, Joey-Bird Carson peeped out from behind a cabin. The mountain displayed its October coloring—the crimson of sumac, the fading blue-black fruit of possum haws, and the dull red-brown of blackberry briers. The scent of wood smoke and the bitter tang of tree bark filled the air.

Papa had a fence built to separate the new grave from the paupers' graveyard. He was about to open the gate for Mrs. Renfrew, but she abruptly placed a gloved hand on the palings to stop him.

Harold Smith had planted ferns and lambkill on the grave. A wooden marker said, "GEORGE RENFREW, August 30, 1907." That was all he and Papa had known to put on it.

"I was going to petition the court to keep him here," Papa said, "but I expect you'll want to have him moved."

She turned abruptly and made her way back to the automobile. Papa followed.

At the vehicle he asked, "He was a doctor?"

"He was," she said.

Papa remembered the wife in Tolstoy's novel who was furious that she had become a widow.

"I'll walk back," he said.

As the automobile moved down the mountain, Papa skirted a field of yellow corn stubble. The woods glowed crimson, scarlet, and rose-gold. The scent of newly cut field corn filled the air. The poor farm's well-kept outbuildings formed a neat cluster around the superintendant's house, built of rosy ballast brick.

It *is* nice here, Papa thought. He had grown up in the valley. Again, he found himself wishing Mr. Renfrew had lived to see the hazelnuts ripen on the ridges. They could have enjoyed it together, taking however long he needed.

As the automobile disappeared, Harold Smith left his men and went to join Papa. His wife had cleaned Mr. Renfrew's cabin and planted a rose bush by its door.

Papa said, "The interesting thing was, she wanted to see where he ended up."

Mr. Smith inspected the cabin's newly whitewashed weatherboarding. "She didn't wear mourning, did she?" he said.

"I didn't reckon she would," Papa said.

Papa said goodnight and set off alone across the fields. Opening and shutting gates, he crossed land that belonged to the poor farm before arriving on our land. At our old horse barn, he placed a hand on its silvery, hand-hewn timbers. The wood still held the heat of the fading day.

It *is* nice here, he thought.

ELI HOOVER

Eli Hoover was a skinny old man with an enormous
Adam's apple. He made a great thing of his saintliness.
I never saw him without his big Bible pressed prominently
against his stomach, which was oddly pointed, as if he had
swallowed a muskmelon and it lodged there, undigested.
His eyes were black and unreflective as a crow's. He wore
a white collarless shirt, its neckband fastened with a simple
gold stud. He wore no tie with his black woolen vest, black
suit jacket, and black pants. A soft black felt hat, at a sedate
angle, covered his bald head. I thought he looked very nice.

Every spring, after the weather warmed up and our
county's dirt roads dried out, he traveled the bumpy mountain roads from his home in Cuyler to visit his "friends."

These "friends" were my family. He had no other
friends that I ever heard of. Most people pretended not to
be home when he came by. Papa's rule, though, was that we
never turned anybody away. That had been the rule in his
own father's family before he married Mama.

As he arrived at our gate, Mr. Hoover said, "Why, 'pon
my soul if it ain't Nellie!" (That was me.) "Wister's oldest
girl, named for your Grandma Nellie McCue—Cody now.
She married Mr. Cody on the thirteenth of January 1874.
The Reverend Abner Sinkler united them over there above
Helmer's Ridge in the Sinklers' old log house." Mr. Hoover
cocked his head and narrowed his black eyes. "A fine lady

your grandma is, too! And since this here day is the first of April 1907, and since your birthday is August twenty-second, you'll be, now let me see..." He paused dramatically. "Now then, you'd be eleven years and eight months and twenty-one days old this very day!"

As Mr. Hoover gave me this news, he set one polished black-shod foot in the lush new grass that sprang up along our broad, freshly whitewashed board fence. He hiked the other foot up against the worn wood of the stile. He never made a mistake in his facts, nor did he ever pause to search his memory or refer to any paper or book. From me, he turned to my brother Dayton.

"'Pon my soul if it ain't Wister's oldest boy!" he exclaimed, staring down into Dayton's intently upturned face. "Named for your Grandpa Dayton Wister—I know that! You used a bad word the last time I stopped by here, and your mammy washed your mouth out with lye soap, ain't that so? And you'll be ten years old on June twenty-fourth!"

Dayton hopped excitedly from foot to foot. He loved being singled out and addressed directly. So did we all. Next, Mr. Hoover turned to our brother Hugh.

"And you're Wister's next boy," he announced, "named for your daddy's oldest brother but one. You favor him, too. *He* lives in Morgantown, and *he* was born on the twelfth of May 1858 at Indian Spring. *You* were born in 1899 on the third day of December at six o'clock in the morning right here in Guthrie County, and you'll be eight years old *this* third of December!"

Skinny, small, red-haired, and freckled, Hugh flushed with pleasure. Behind him, skipping in her excitement, our sister Bess came over to greet Mr. Hoover as well.

He didn't disappoint her.

"And here's Wister's next-to-oldest girl," he declared, "named for your mama's music teacher Miss Bess Showalter.

You wasn't but a puny little thing the day you was born, and now look at you! *You*'ll be six the third of August."

Like the Pied Piper, Mr. Hoover eased his way forward through a clot of admiring children. Our sister Lily, small, green-eyed, and shy, stared out at him through the kitchen's closed screen door.

"And I do declare if it ain't Lily!" he said as he hoisted his bony frame up onto the porch. "Named for your aunt who was killed by lightning on the eighth of July 1899. *She* was born on the seventeenth of September 1879, and *you*," he squinted down at Lily's serious little upturned face, "you was born on January twelfth, four years and two months and nineteen days ago this Sunday next!"

In a day when children were seen but not heard, it was thrilling being addressed separately and elaborately by an adult.

Behind Lily, our hired girls were less impressed. Mr. Hoover pushed his way into the overheated kitchen.

Squinting through clouds of steam at our oldest hired woman, he declared loudly, "'Pon my soul if it ain't Mrs. Pennybacker! I mind well the day the Lord sent Mr. Wister down to Back Creek by Simms's Mountain and found you and your four little ones starving. That was the tenth of June 1903, four years and two months and ten days ago today! Now, let me see, your two youngest are Frank and Verdie, and they reside at the poor farm. And Elsie, she works for Neffs, and Andy, he helps Dan Kefaver, the peg-leg man who carries the mail!"

Mrs. Pennybacker, her hands white with flour, grimaced and kept her eyes on the stove. Her young helper Ola Smith fixed her large, pale-lashed eyes on Mr. Hoover.

"Why, if it ain't Jim Smith's oldest girl!" the old man told Ola. "With the Wisters two years now this August, ain't that so? Now, you came here August fifteenth 1905. And you was born February twelfth 1890, and that was a dark night for your poor mammy, may the Lord rest her soul!"

After greeting our hired girls, Mr. Hoover edged himself around the big dining table and threaded his way out the far doorway to the rest of the house. His aim was the front porch.

Bess detached herself from the crush of admiring children who followed and scooted past him to the sitting room. "Mama!" she cried, "Mr. Hoover's here!"

Without looking up from the collar she was turning on one of Papa's shirts, Mama said coolly, "Yes. Well, I suppose he is."

Her impressions of Mr. Hoover came from her mother. Grandma Cody had said, (unfairly, I thought), "The cultivation of his memory is the only work that old hypocrite ever did in his life." Whenever I think about Mr. Hoover, I wonder at the long hours he must have spent down there in Cuyler, in the dead of winter, studying over the facts of my family's lives. Then, when the snow melted and the roads dried out, he and his old horse could make their way down to us so he could spend days eating our food and sleeping in one of our feather beds. He'd earn his keep by telling us all about ourselves.

On the front porch, Mr. Hoover chose a green-painted rocking chair for himself.

Papa, sitting in his own green chair, looked up. "Why, Eli, what brings you here?"

"I've come to see my friends," Mr. Hoover said with dignity.

"I expect you'll stay long enough to eat with us," Papa said.

For some reason I never fathomed, Mr. Hoover never recited Papa's biography to him.

When Ola came through the house clanging the bell for supper, Mr. Hoover rose and followed Papa to the dining room. He drew out and sat in the chair on Papa's right.

Once we were all seated, he bowed his head and squeezed his eyes shut. "Lord, we thank Thee for multiplying the fortunes of this fine family," he prayed, "and for making them so generous to those who are weary and faint of heart..." and so on.

He blessed Mama and Papa, and each of us children, and each of our hired men and women, and all our tenants, and if we had any guests, them, too. When he finished his blessings, the food was cold.

At last, he opened his eyes and fixed them on Mama. "Members of the fair sex don't like to hear their ages told," he said, "so I'll just say there was no moon the night your mammy sent for your Grandma McCue to come quick! I'll just say it was October, the same night the youngest Ratliff child wandered off from the poor farm."

The Ratliff child was not talked about at our house. It was the depths of winter when his frozen body was discovered.

Mama sent a meaning look down the table. To change the subject, she asked Papa, "Is it this week or next that the men are coming for the cattle, Jack?"

"This week," Papa answered. He looked amused.

"The night the Didrick infant died, in fact..." Mr. Hoover plunged on. We children were thrilled to hear this sad tale as well. No one except Mr. Hoover ever mentioned such events in our presence. The Didrick child had died of fever, some said, or of neglect, said others.

Mr. Hoover snaked out a skinny arm, drew in a big bowl of butterbeans, and helped himself liberally. He then turned his attention to the ham, gravy, creamed corn, corn-bread, applesauce, apple butter, damson jam, and slaw. We children got a chance to see something else that fascinated us. With every swallow, his Adam's apple jumped as if a string were attached to it and someone gave it a series of sudden, violent jerks.

After supper, Papa and Mr. Hoover returned to the porch. It grew dark, and Mama sent us children out to say goodnight. The gilded edges of Mr. Hoover's big Bible glinted in the yellow lamplight from the sitting room window.

As we children appeared, he struck his forehead with the flat of his palm. "Why, 'pon my soul! How time does fly! And here I studied on getting home before dark! 'Pon my *soul*, my *horse*!"

Papa smiled. "Your horse has been fed, Eli. She's in the barn. And as for you, there's bound to be an extra bed somewhere in this old house."

The next morning, and the next and the next, Mr. Hoover sat on our porch enjoying the view. He looked out over the rich, level fields of river bottomland and the mountains beyond. He admired Papa's new barn and read his Bible.

One year, during one of Mr. Hoover's visits, a stranger came by. Seeing Mr. Hoover on our porch, he exclaimed, "Why, Eli Hoover, you old sinner!"

Mr. Hoover didn't answer, and the stranger laughed— an odd laugh, I thought.

"Mr. Wister," the stranger said, turning to Papa, "have you ever heard this saintly man here cuss? You haven't? Why, I used to work for him. I must have been eleven, twelve maybe, cheap help for him. He used to put me up for the night so we could get an early start at our work. One such night, something woke me out of a sound sleep. I threw back the quilts and ran to the window. Directly below me, under a pear tree, was old Eli in his nightshirt, shaking his fist, cussing a blue streak. I mean *cussing*! I never knew such words existed! An owl had made off with one of his hens that roosted in that tree. Why, Mr. Wister, I was shocked. I'd always seen him carrying that big Bible and reading out of it and praying at meetings...If there was more to this story, my brothers and sisters and I never heard it; it was time for us to go to bed.

But we did manage to hear the stranger say, "You remember that, don't you, Eli?" We could tell Mr. Hoover was not happy.

"I don't remember," he said faintly.

When my sister Bess grew up, she married a man from Cuyler. He told another story. One night, Mr. Hoover showed up at his house. His mother, a widow with seven small children, had made a kettle of soup for their supper. Mr. Hoover pulled out a seat at her table and wedged himself in amongst the children. He then drank all the soup. When he was done, without a drop of apology or shame, he said, "'Pon my soul, Dellie, I do believe these children are hungry."

Left to right, Grandma Cody, Mama, and Bess Wister

BESS WISTER

Every spring, Mama dosed us children with santonin, a patent cure for intestinal worms, and calomel, a purgative. My sister Bess, age seven, dragged a chair up to the medicine shelf to get the pills down. She assembled them with glasses of water and oranges, our traditional pill-taking treat. On her orders, my brothers and sisters and I stood waiting while she set off to find Mama. We were not pleased to be hounded from bed at sunup and ordered about like cattle, yet not one of us dared cross her.

Bess worked so fast that she often made comical mistakes. On Sundays, for instance, when she got us ready for church, Elsie's right shoe could be on her left foot, Lily's drawers could be unattached to her vest, and Bess's own braids could be lopsided—one fat, the other thin.

But we were ready, weren't we? Mama was going to be surprised!

Bess had Mama's thick, glossy dark hair, lovely brown eyes, and amazing energy. She also had the brisk, no-nonsense manner of an army drill sergeant. After she got us ready for church, she proceeded to the dining room and dragged out Mama's best damask tablecloth. She laid it, not quite straight and without its protective pad, on the table.

Mama always made a show of being pleased with all this. "Who can have set the table so nicely?" she said, then moved the knives and forks to their proper places. "How pretty it looks!"

An itinerant photographer arrived every spring to take our pictures. Bess always spotted him before anyone else. One time, she got us into our clothes and strung us out across the porch, our newest baby sister in her arms. The only trouble was, she hadn't given us time to put on our shoes.

There we were, weren't we? Mama was going to be surprised!

My brother Dayton happened to be the first to see the finished print. "Looky here, Bess," he said. "Nellie and I are the only ones who have our shoes on."

Bess gave him a look reserved for perfectionists. "We have the picture, don't we?"

Two boys came to our farm with their father. They brought corn to be ground into grists. One boy, about four years old, sat on their horse behind their father. His brother, a year or two older, dawdled along on foot, whacking off clover heads with a hickory switch.

As their father set off to find our hired man, he told the boys, "Now, don't neither one of you young'uns move off these here steps."

Bess had seen them arrive. "What's your name?" she demanded of the older one. She looked at his brother. "What's *his* name?"

Names were vital to a bossy girl like my sister. How could she order these boys around if she didn't know what to call them? Neither boy spoke or even looked in her direction. The dinner bell rang. Bess scrambled to her feet and ran into the house. After dinner, she tried again, but the boys never so much as raised their eyes.

When the boys grew old enough to come alone for their grists, they arrived at our kitchen fence and sat silently on their old horse until somebody noticed them. Then the oldest said gruffly, "We come fer a grist fer Pa." Our hired man watered the mare and produced their grist. With no further words, the boys rode off again.

One day, they appeared with a tiny brother, towheaded like them and solemn as a circuit judge. As they sat on the granary steps, Bess arrived and asked her usual questions, with the usual results.

Once, when the boys were there, somebody told Mama. She loaded a tray with food and gave it to me to carry, and she filled a pitcher with milk and gave it to Bess. As we approached the granary steps with our burdens, the boys looked at us for the first time.

From the moment Bess began her campaign to make the boys talk, we never doubted she'd succeed.

Looking at the oldest boy, she said, "What's your name?"

"Hit's Coy," he answered.

"What's *his* name?"

"Hit's Harness."

"And what's *his* name?"

"We call him Jur-ry."

Bess handed over her pitcher. I set down my tray.

At the kitchen door, I overheard Bess announce to the men at the dinner table, "Their names are Coy, Harness, and Jur-ry."

In time, the oldest of the boys arrived to work for us. Bess overheard our hired men address him as "Dan'l." She gave them a reproving look.

"His name is Coy," she corrected them.

"'T ain't," he corrected her. "Hit's Dan'l."

"What's your brother's name?" Bess said.

"Hit's Lester."

"And what's your other brother's name?

"Hit's Furness."

Whenever a member of our family is asked his name, one of us answers hoarsely, "We call him Jur-ry."

Bess dismisses this, pretending not to remember the incident.

Bess was ten when she went to work for a mail-order company that rewarded its farmwife saleswomen with bonuses of china and glassware. Bess's goal, as usual, was to surprise Mama.

Mama stipulated that she not approach our hired men or women, that she go no farther up the road than the poor farm, and that our brother Dayton accompany her.

Our neighbors ordered tooth powder, tea, vanilla extracts, stove blacking, laundry bluing, healing salves, and remedies for poultry diseases.

A woman, new to the valley, allowed Bess to rattle off her prepared speech. She then said, "Your folks can buy you anything you want," and slammed the door in her face.

Bess was not offended; she just carried on. Dayton was outraged, as were the rest of us children when we heard the story.

Bess surprised Mama with the bonuses won from the mail-order company. There was a forty-four-piece set of Johnson Brothers china dishes painted with forget-me-nots. Also included were six iridescent, plum-colored, pressed-glass cups and saucers. As was the fashion at the time, the glassware was imprinted with a rhyme: "When next you brew a cup of tea, drink it down and think of me."

Bess grew up to become a nurse. Her bossy side made her a superb nurse, but in her private life, she was still oddly eccentric. She married a doctor, a reserved, almost silent, man who loved her dearly. I visited them once in the small town where they practiced medicine until he retired.

He and I took a walk one evening. He had suffered a stroke and was very frail. As we walked slowly past a magnificent magnolia tree, a woman leaned over her porch railing and snipped off an enormous, fragrant blossom.

"It's a treat to see you out and about, Doctor," she told him. She gave me a sly smile and whispered to me, "Without your sister."

My brother-in-law broke his accustomed silence. "Your sister is a saint," he told me as we walked on. "I'd never have made it without her."

MRS. PENNYBACKER

Around the end of March or early April I sometimes saw a small, dumpy figure trudging up our farm lane. "Mrs. Pennybacker!" I shouted. "Frankie's here!"

Frankie Pennybacker moved so slowly it was hard to be sure he was really in motion. He fumbled the gate latch open, turned himself around, and backed through the opening. Mrs. Pennybacker hurried out. She took his chubby hand in hers and helped him climb onto the big porch bench. She examined his clothing and ran a hand through his hair. She wanted to know how Mrs. Smith at the poor farm was keeping him. She never brought him inside our house.

"Now, Frankie, you stay right there," she said. "I'm going to bring you a cookie."

Meanwhile, my brothers scurried off to find our hired man, who hitched up the buggy to drive Frankie back to the poor farm, a mile or so up the road.

"I'll see you and Verdie Saturday," Mrs. Pennybacker promised Frankie. His sister Verdie usually sat in a heap, with her mouth open, on the poor farm's porch. She never went anywhere.

Papa found Mrs. Pennybacker living in a house about to be sold for taxes. Her husband had died. As Guthrie County's commissioner for the poor, Papa placed Frankie and

Verdie in the poor farm and found private homes for her two normal children. We always needed help, so he brought Mrs. Pennybacker to live with us.

From the time I was six, in 1901, until I was fifteen, Mrs. Pennybacker lived with us as our housekeeper. She always dressed in a long-sleeved blue dress with a blue-and-white-checked gingham apron. Around her neck she wore a blue bandanna kerchief with its ends knotted, always on the same side, to hide her goiter. "She must have been pretty before she had that growth," I'd overheard Mama say. Goiters were common before doctors understood the importance of iodine in the diet.

Every afternoon Mrs. Pennybacker, who worked hard all day, was supposed to rest. Instead, she searched through the old-clothes-basket in Mama's room for socks to mend, towels to re-hem, or a shirt of Papa's that needed its collar reversed.

Mama said, "Oh, Sally, go lie down."

"It rests me to have something to do, Mrs. Wister," she said.

Mama, seeing her on her way to the garden, said, "Oh, Sally, the *men* will do *that.*"

"I like to get outdoors, Mrs. Wister," Mrs. Pennybacker replied. "Picking bean beetles rests me."

Mrs. Pennybacker had clear, very white skin, black hair, and black eyes. She must have been in her late twenties. One of her favorite ways of "resting" was to take us children berry picking. She asked Papa where the blackberries were plentiful that year. He'd say, "Above our tenant house, along our line fence, or near the springhouse." She'd pull heavy woolen stockings, with the feet cut out, over my sister's small arms and legs to protect her from rattlesnakes and copperheads. She handed out stockings for us older children to put on. She made sure each one of us had a straw hat and a tin cup to pick into. She herself carried a woven two-peck basket and a half-gallon tin bucket. Rolled in a towel around her waist were a sharp knife and a bottle of turpentine for snakebites. A sack held a picnic of buttered bread and cucumbers. Up past our big barn we went, chattering like sparrows.

At the springhouse, Mrs. Pennybacker let down her bucket. Avoiding minnows, tadpoles, and crawdads, she lifted it up, dripping with cold, clear water to take along.

She chose blackberry bushes with heavy crops for us children.

"Dayton, here's one for you," she said. "Hugh, here's yours. Bess, this one's yours." Dayton, Hugh, and Bess filled their cups with leaves and covered them with a layer of berries.

Mrs. Pennybacker winked at me.

"Is anybody hungry?" she asked.

In the shade of one of the big white oak trees that followed our line fence, we ate our picnic and some of the berries we'd picked. In the valley below, our farmhouse and its outbuildings looked like a toy village. On the clear, bright air, the Neffs' dinner bell clanged faintly and, almost simultaneously, so did ours. Seconds later, the Floods' bell rang. In the fields below the road, the men looked as tiny as ants converging on the lanes, headed home to dinner.

Because we were only children, Mrs. Pennybacker took off her kerchief. Her goiter was as big as a goose egg. In spite of it, we thought her beautiful.

By two o'clock, it was time to go home so she could begin fixing supper.

Mrs. Pennybacker made our berries into cobblers. Dinner the next day consisted of cobbler—fragrant with burnt sugar and oozing purple juice—served with sweetened milk called "dip." We ate from bowls using soupspoons. Nothing else was on the table, just pans of cobbler and china pitchers filled with dip.

Mama paid Mrs. Pennybacker a dollar a week and gave her clothing and whatever else she needed. The back of the upstairs hall was her province and out of bounds to us children. She shared it with Ola Smith.

Every Saturday, Mrs. Pennybacker scoured the kitchen floor with pounded sandstone and lye soap. She blacked the kitchen range and polished its nickel trim. She helped us children grease our Sunday shoes and lay out our clothes for church. She cooked ahead for Sunday dinner. On Saturday afternoon, Ola Smith's father came for her from across the mountain. Mrs. Pennybacker went to see her children at the poor farm. She rode our mare Pansy, looking very different from her everyday self. Instead of her blue bandana, she wore a black silk kerchief with a black bonnet over it. Her dress, also black silk, boasted many tiny rows of stitching. She wore black kid gloves. Her black hair escaped around her forehead. She moved in a whiff of lavender.

We children watched her uneasily. *Would she come back?*

One rainy Sunday, Papa was preparing to fetch her in the buggy.

Dayton shouted excitedly, "Come see! Papa, come see!"

A strange buggy was making its way up our lane. Riding in the passenger seat was our own Mrs. Pennybacker. Beside her, driving a magnificent black gelding, was a man we had never seen before. Pansy trotted along behind. Mrs. Pennybacker hopped down at our gate. Without a word, she entered the kitchen and disappeared up to her room. At a nod from Papa, Dayton took Pansy to the barn. The stranger tipped his hat to Papa and drove away.

The following Saturday, our hired man saddled Pansy.

Mrs. Pennybacker said, "Thank you, Reuben, I have a ride."

Within moments, the strange buggy reappeared. Its driver, the same tall man, wearing a brown suit and carrying a brown hat, came to the door.

"This is Mr. Fox, children," Mrs. Pennybacker told us and introduced each one of us.

After that, we children watched her closely. She cooked and cleaned as usual. She helped us grease our shoes and prepare our clothes for school and church. She took us to pick huckleberries and, as the weather turned cold, to hunt beechnuts and pawpaws.

"Sally's friend is Harold Smith's cousin, Carrie," Papa told Mama. "He is a bachelor. That little farm, up behind the Dunkard church, is his." (Harold Smith was the superintendent of the poor farm.)

"He won't want her children, Jack," Mama said. "A man wants a family of his own."

One Sunday evening, as we were gathered in the sitting room, there was a rap on the door. There stood Mrs. Pennybacker and her new friend.

"Mr. Fox and I are going to be married," she told us.

Papa took Mr. Fox to his office to talk.

Later, he told Mama, "He'll be good for her. He'll make her a good husband."

For a wedding present, I embroidered Mrs. Pennybacker's monogram on a pair of pillow shams. Dayton and Hugh used money they had earned snaring rabbits in the orchard to buy her a pressed-glass butter dish. I helped Bess sew a length of store-bought lace onto a handkerchief.

Bess refused to believe Mrs. Pennybacker would leave us. "What will Mr. Fox do when he sees her goiter?"

The day of Mrs. Pennybacker's departure, she stood in our kitchen wearing a new navy-blue coat and a matching hat Mama had bought for her. She carried a leather pocketbook and a traveling case. Papa gave her a hundred dollars, which, in those days, could buy a nine-piece set of solid-walnut dining room furniture, or a mahogany piano with ebony and ivory keys, or a road wagon for Mr. Fox's farm. Then she was gone.

In 1910, she came to see us, carrying a two-year-old boy named Owen, which was Mr. Fox's given name.

Noticing my worried expression, she smiled and assured me, "He's fine, Nellie. *Really*, he is."

Bess, who had been born the year Mrs. Pennybacker came to work for us, never gave her the wedding present I helped her make. She never forgave her for leaving us.

HARRY JEFFERSON

When I was a little girl one of our farm hands was color-blind. My little brothers and I had never heard of this affliction. We spent a lot of time testing him.

"What color is *that*, Harry?" We pointed to the blue graniteware coffee pot that sat on the kitchen range.

"Gray?" Harry guessed. "Green?"

"And what color's *this*?" Dayton asked.

"Blue?" Harry guessed.

"*No*!" Dayton crowed. "It's *yellow*!"

A time came when Harry remembered the colors of the things we pointed to. "You see," he said, "I ain't such a bad case as you kids make out."

The other thing we found interesting about him was that he was "colored," as we said in those days. His hair was kinky and his mother, Mary Ann Jefferson, had very dark skin.

"What color is your skin, Harry?" Dayton asked.

"Same as yours," he answered good-naturedly. "Skin color."

A girl who worked for us claimed it was dangerous to say Harry was "colored." "If your Mama hears that she'll tan your little bottoms," Becky said.

Every evening after Harry finished his farmwork, he took his banjo and walked down to the "hill," as we said. This in itself was interesting to us children. Our other hired men sat in the kitchen with the hired girls before climbing wearily to their rooms, sometimes even while it was still light. They were middle-aged men. Harry was seventeen.

"Now just because my back is turned, don't you kids think you can get up to something I wouldn't approve of," Harry told us as he set off for the hill.

"One of these here days, he's a-going to get hisself in trouble," Becky said darkly.

The very next morning Harry appeared at the breakfast table sporting a black eye. Parker Finch, a man old enough to be Harry's father, winked at the other men.

Harry defended himself. "One of the fellas was swingin' a cane around, and the end came off and hit me."

Papa said, "Don't worry about Harry. He's just sowing a few wild oats."

One Sunday after dinner Mama was resting and Papa was away. The men and women who worked for us, including Harry, spent Sundays with their families. Except for a fly buzzing on the flypaper roll hanging from the kitchen ceiling, the house was silent. My brothers and I were playing "farmer," using red-and-white corncobs as Hereford cattle.

Dayton said abruptly, "I bet you Harry's got a bottle in his room."

One of Mama's firmest rules was that we children were never, ever, for any reason, to go into the hired-men's room. I figured, though, that if we did and, as Dayton argued, found a bottle, wouldn't Mama be pleased? Up the stairs I ran, on Dayton's heels, followed by Hugh.

A packing crate served as Harry's bedside table. Affixed to the wall was a piece of looking glass. A hickory-cotton shirt and denim overalls hung from nails. On the bed lay a celluloid comb and a pack of playing cards.

In our house, playing cards were bad, indeed. Our Methodist grandmother kept a book that described the terrible fates of card-players as well as drinkers. Surely, we thought, Mama would praise us for taking Harry's cards. Dayton made a dash into the room and snatched up the cards.

We fled back down the stairs, our search for corn liquor forgotten, and out into the yard we ran. We hurried past the parlor chimney and the corner of the front porch. Under the snowball bush, at the foot of the lawn, we tore the cards to bits. Then we raced back to the house.

Dayton and Hugh may have headed for the barn, a logical place for farm-bred boys to examine their consciences. I sat in my room, having serious second thoughts about our adventure.

The next morning, Mama shepherded us into her room.

"What do you know about *these*?" she asked, showing us five or six bits of torn cardboard.

I believed she'd say we'd done a good thing. To my horror, she turned me over her knee and spanked me.

"Going into Harry's room was wrong," she said. "Taking his property was very wrong." She let me go, then gave Dayton and Hugh their turns.

At supper, Harry greeted us children with his usual, easygoing "Hi, kids, what did you get up to today?"

The next morning, we overheard Papa congratulate Harry on finding work in Keyser.

A week later, he appeared, carrying his banjo and a cardboard suitcase.

"Don't you believe every good-looking feller who comes along, Bess," he said, giving her a broad wink. He turned to us children. "When I make my fortune, I'll come back here and tell you kids about it."

The next thing we knew, he was gone.

One winter morning, Harry's mother appeared in our warm kitchen to wait for her kettles in the washhouse to boil.

"You know, Harry, he got him a job in Keyser," she told us. "He's a brakeman on the railroad."

"What's a brakeman?" Dayton wanted to know.

"He stops the trains."

"How does he know when to stop them?"

"There's signals," Mary Ann explained. "They're different colors. When the color changes, he waves a flag."

We were horrified.

Didn't the railroad know Harry was color-blind? What would happen if he mixed up the signals? What if he caused a wreck?

"People might get killed," said Dayton to me privately that evening. "If Harry mixes up the colors and gives the wrong signal...*lots* of people could get killed. We have to tell the railroad that he's color-blind."

"We better stay out of it," I said. "Remember what happened last time?"

"This is different. What if there was a wreck and we could have stopped it?"

My handwriting was better than Dayton's, so I wrote a short letter and addressed it to the railroad:

Dear Sirs,

One of your brakemen, Mr. Harry Jefferson, is color-blind.

Yours truly,

A concerned citizen

At the foot of the lawn, our large mailbox held a stout canvas bag for outgoing mail. Dayton untied the mailbag's strings.

"Put it in," he said.

"*You* put it in," I said.

"Put it in!" he insisted, glancing down the road. "The stage is coming."

"Once I put it in, it's gone." I said.

We remembered the playing cards incident and the spankings we'd gotten.

A light sparked in my brother's eyes.

"Wait!" he said. "Don't put it in. Tear it up! I *know* what happened—a doctor gave Harry some medicine. He's cured! A big railroad like that would never give that job to a color-blind man."

"You could be right," I agreed.

Dayton snatched the letter and ripped it up.

Without a word, we crossed the road and climbed over the fence into the cornfield. There, we buried the evidence.

Nellie Wister

DR. JOHN ECHOLS

*B*lasts *From the Ram's Horn* was a book that figured
prominently in my family's parlor bookcase. Published
in 1902, it had belonged to my Methodist grandmother. I
remember every one of its illustrations.

Young men peer into saloon windows at fat publicans
wearing aprons labeled "Vice." Subsequently, the same young
men reel away, their clothes awry. A wolfish cur named
"License" snarls at their heels.

Fashionably dressed men, with skulls' faces, embrace
innocent, young brides. Helmeted, virginal young women
flourish flaming brands in defense of children. The same
wolfish cur, "License," slavers at their heels.

Pilgrims pause before a dark "Cavern Of Doubt,"
inside of which are volumes entitled Renen, Huxley, Scho-
penhauer, and Darwin. Satan offers the pilgrims a stone
inscribed "Materialism."

Rabbles of men trail after leaders labeled "Saloon Politics," waving signs that read, "We Are The Voters." Women
and children with wasted features represent "Non-Voters."

A billy goat in a cutaway coat and top hat and a fat-jew-
eled sow ride in an elegant carriage. The winking, smartly uniformed driver is Satan. This drawing is titled "At The Races."

The margins are crowded with spiders, snakes, bats,
and death's heads. Wee, fashionably dressed gentlemen and
ladies dance to the fiddling of skeletons.

When I was five years old and hadn't yet learned to read, I asked Mama to read the texts to me.

"When you're older," she said. With that, the fascinating volume disappeared. A Presbyterian, she disapproved of this Methodist tract.

I was sixteen when my maternal grandmother introduced me to Dr. John Echols, a young man she had vetted especially for me. A native of Virginia, he was a graduate of Virginia Military Institute and the medical school at the University of Virginia.

Grandma winked at me across the dinner table. "Did you see his horse?" she whispered. "A beautiful black gelding named 'Traveler,' for General Lee's horse."

I wasn't interested in horses. I was interested in him. He was strikingly handsome and had an air of authority.

"He isn't married, Nellie!" Grandma whispered.

Papa introduced Dr. Echols into our community and helped him find an office in Mr. Hugh Kimble's house. Dr. Echols cured one of my schoolmates of cramp colic. He cured members of the Probst family of diphtheria. He brought in a special nurse to look after the youngest Neff girl when she came down with typhoid fever.

He told Eula Conrad, who had a bladder infection, to pour water out of one bucket into another, as the sound would encourage her to void. "Well, my Lord," he said impatiently to Eula's mother, "she knows how to do *that*, doesn't she? Tell her to hold a warm damp rag against herself and urinate through that."

The doctor's use of anatomical verbs, as well as his occasional use of the Lord's name in vain, horrified Eula's mother. But other ladies with marriageable daughters invited him to dinner. Increasingly, he begged off their invitations to dine with Grandma and me. Often, during these dinners, Grandma found reasons to leave us alone to give us time to talk. He was marvelously educated, both scholastically and by experience, and was courtly and immaculately respectful.

Grandma's friend Mrs. Nash went to the doctor's office one day to find it locked. The landlord hadn't seen him that day and assumed some emergency had called him away.

A noise inside aroused her curiosity. She cupped an eye to the keyhole. She saw the doctor slumped in a chair, his usually neat suit looking as if he had slept in it, and he had a growth of beard.

What a terrible emergency that must have been! she thought. *What a fine doctor he was!*

Then she smelled corn liquor all the way out on the porch.

Grandma was horrified at the story. The doctor, whom she had worked so hard to arrange for me, was a common drunk. But Papa believed every man deserved a second chance. I agreed. The doctor was still the handsomest man in the county. To me, his failing made him more alluring, even a touch dangerous. I found it a relief that he wasn't perfect. At last, and under protest, Grandma agreed to invite him to dinner again.

One day, in the schoolyard, my friend Maud Flood grabbed my arm. "Look! Nellie! Look!" she cried. Across the road came the beautiful black gelding, stepping carefully, its reins slack, with Dr. Echols in the saddle. The horse, of its own accord, stopped at the schoolhouse gate.

Our teacher, just out of school himself, laid a hand on its bridle. "Doc," he whispered, "hadn't you better go on home?"

The doctor swept off his hat. "Patient up on the creek," he muttered. "Mus' go."

With that, Traveler turned and ambled off toward Duncan's Creek.

Later that same day, Maud and I saw the doctor, swaying loosely in the saddle, riding back from Duncan's Creek. Traveler moved slowly and cautiously.

Seeing the doctor in that condition, and in front of my schoolmates, deeply shocked and embarrassed me. It stripped away any romantic ideas I may have had about his failing.

Mr. Cecil McComas was a white-bearded old soldier who had had two horses shot from under him at the Battle of Sharpsburg. He always spoke as if he were shouting over cannon fire. He and his bachelor son lived across the road from the doctor. One night, they awoke to a sound that came from their hired girl's room. Mr. McComas and his son knocked at the girl's door. Getting no answer, they opened the door. There, in the light of their lamp, was Dr. Echols—in bed with her.

"Great day in the morning!" Mr. McComas bellowed.

Three days later, Dr. Echols appeared at our door. He begged my forgiveness. I left the room without speaking to him. It was Grandma who showed him out.

Papa paid him a visit. He was, after all, the one who had encouraged the doctor to settle among us. The "Keeley cure," he said, was a pioneering treatment for alcoholism. Called quackery by some and miraculous by others, it involved the administration of strychnine, apomorphine, ammonia, atropine, willow bark, and bichloride of gold.

"Cure!" the doctor exclaimed, running a shaky hand through his hair. "Well, my Lord, I need a cure!" While Dr. Echols went to take the Keeley cure, I went away to boarding school.

Mama considered Dr. Echols a fine example to local drinkers. Her brother was a drinker. The doctor had faced up to his weakness and overcome it. She invited him to dinner. It was Christmas, and I was home.

Grandma, still not convinced, seated the doctor as far from me as she could.

He called down the table, "Nellie, how do you like school?"

"I love it!" I raised my voice. "Lewisburg is a beautiful town!"

"I have family there," he shouted over the increasing clamor of dishes and conversation. "Do you know them?"

"Your niece is in my class," I shouted.

Any further conversation was futile over the din of the holiday meal.

After Lewisburg, I took a job teaching school in Monroe County. The United States entered the First World War. My brother Dayton joined the Army and so did Dr. Echols. Dayton wrote me from his training camp. Dr. Echols wrote from the battlefield. He sent me presents of silk scarves embroidered with scarlet poppies and the names "Flanders,"

"Marne," and "Ypres." He sent a German officer's helmet pierced by bullets and an enormous polished-brass shell casing, with an incised design of lilies and the name "Verdun." He sent photographs of himself at his field hospital. His letters—short, neat, and concise—arrived regularly. I felt proud to correspond with an officer who served abroad.

When the war ended, the doctor and my brother came home on almost the same day. One noontime, I found myself at the dinner table, again with Dr. Echols. Years had passed since he'd subjected himself to the Keeley cure. By all accounts, he hadn't been drunk since. He was handsome and deeply tanned. He had his old, fine military bearing. I had decided I wanted to be a nurse, but Papa disapproved of my ambition. To my surprise, Dr. Echols agreed. Nursing was menial work, he said. On the other hand, I was encouraged when he said that there was a definite need for good nurses. He said he was sure I'd do well if I really decided to go into it.

After dinner, he asked me to accompany him into the parlor. We sat across from each other at a low table. He took two small blue-velvet-covered boxes from a breast pocket and laid them in front of me. Inside one was a rosy cameo brooch set in a rich, dark-yellow-gold filigree. The second contained a beautiful ring set with a rose-cut yellow sapphire.

"I bought these in Italy," he said. "The ring is just your size. I'd be honored if you'd be my wife."

I knew Mama would be pleased if I said yes. I knew Grandma would be appalled. As for Papa, he and everyone in the valley admired the doctor's skills, especially that he had overcome his affliction.

But had he? Did anyone ever really overcome that weakness? Did it lie dormant?

At that moment, on the shelf behind the doctor, I saw a familiar title—*Blasts From the Ram's Horn*. There the old book was again, after so many years. A vision rose before me: saloon doors swung wide; innocent young men peering in; fat, leering saloonkeepers lurking there; and serpents, spiders, and Satan himself.

In a flash, I remembered my teacher from long ago, his hand on the bridle of the doctor's beautiful black gelding. I heard him whisper, *Doc, don't you think you'd better go on home?*

I closed the lids of the two small boxes and slid them across the table. "They're beautiful," I said, "but I can't accept them."

"Is there someone else?"

"There is no one else," I said.

He sighed deeply, rose to his feet, and slipped the two boxes into his breast pocket. Grandma showed him to the door.

JANE HAMRICK

A grove of chestnut trees separated Mr. Saul McComas's wheat field from a patch of blackberry briars and red brush where Jane Hamrick lived.

Jane was very tall and dressed always in rusty black. She wore high-topped, many-buttoned back boots; a lace-trimmed black apron; a black poke bonnet; and long, full, black skirts. Old ladies in our part of West Virginia wore such clothing during the War Between the States and long afterward. If you saw Jane in a dim light or from a distance, you might think you saw a ghost; she walked so oddly, gliding along close to Mr. McComas's fences. Small children were afraid of her; teenage boys ran after her and hooted.

Jane had fifteen children by fifteen different men. The children were all grown and gone, and she was long past the age of having more. She shared her cabin with a dozen dogs, cats, and chickens, the chief of which was a rooster named Cecil.

Cecil was a big rusty-red bird with an enormous, floppy, red comb and metallic-purple tail feathers that swept the ground. He was full of good cheer for the life he lived with Jane. He never let her out his sight. When she drew water from Mr. McComas's well or chopped wood for her fire, he followed her. She worked two days a week for Mrs. McComas and two for my Grandma Cody. Cecil watched

Jane while she washed Grandma's laundry from an apple tree outside the dusty window of the little washhouse.

As Jane cooked, Cecil sat on top of the wood box and kept an eye on her for tidbits. Jane collected the eggs laid by his many wives and carried them in a split-oak basket to Mr. Morgan Armistead's store. There, she traded them for Diamond dye, poultry dip, and molasses. The boys, who hung around the store, flapped their arms and crowed at her.

One day, Jane found Cecil standing with his legs wide apart, his neck stretched forward, gasping. She tried to fish out whatever was caught in his throat, but only managed to push it deeper. As night fell, she carried Cecil up the hill, past the schoolhouse, to my Uncle Pent's.

Uncle Pent placed Cecil on his operating table and handed Jane an oil lamp. Using a small instrument, he pulled out a tiny piece of wire. Right away, Cecil jumped up, puffed up his beautiful feathers, stretched out his neck, and crowed.

"I *knowed* you could cure him, Doctor!" Jane exclaimed.

The oldest Waybright boys, Dr. John Hunter's sons, and Royce and Baxter Flood saw Jane leave Uncle Pent's. They flapped their arms and crowed.

The next day, she appeared in Mr. Armistead's store and bought a Hopkins and Allen shotgun and a box of buckshot. When the boys gathered again to tease her, she flung open the cabin door and fired.

Claud Waybright's father appeared at Mr. McComas's door to complain.

"I'm sorry Claud got hurt," Mr. McComas said, "but there's no excuse for a fellow his age teasing a woman like Jane. She never did him any harm, did she?"

That night, instead of lecturing Claud, Mr. Waybright thrashed him.

Generations of boys continued to flap their arms and crow at Jane. Armistead's store became Caudle's. Jane's great-granddaughter arrived at the cabin to look after her. One of Cecil's descendants, with his forebear's gorgeous metallic tail feathers, took to following *her.*

She was a short-tempered fat woman with no sense of humor whatsoever.

No one ever teased *her.*

MARY HANNAH

Dice Cody's wife died one evening in June. The next afternoon I carried a bowl of Mama's potato salad up to his house. I found Teenie Hardesty in the kitchen.

Drying her hands on her apron, she followed me out onto the back porch. "The others are going home after supper, Nellie," she whispered. (Mrs. Neff and Mrs. Flood had helped lay out Mary Hannah Cody's body that morning.) "Will you come back and help me sit up with her?"

I hadn't known Mary Hannah Cody very well and I barely knew Dice. I had never sat up with a dead person. I couldn't really say I knew Teenie. She was married, while I was just sixteen. In 1911, in a small place like Chinkapin Creek, when somebody died, you did as much as you could. Miss Jenny Bowles took Mary Hannah's little boy in to stay with her until Dice could get back on his feet. Miss Fan Swisher had her hired girl make a custard pie. I knew Mama would want me to help Teenie. She said she wanted me after supper and asked if I would stay till midnight.

Mama said, "Take the Overland, Nellie." I'd been driving since I was twelve. Unlike our old Ford, which started by hand crank, the Overland had an ignition. I could manage that on my own.

I helped our hired girls clean up the supper things and then drove to Dice's.

As I drove into the lane, Joe Flood came chugging up behind me in his mother's Maxwell.

As we left the automobiles, he said, "Teenie asked me to sit up with you-all."

I said I was glad of that. Once it started to get dark and Dice's little house got quiet, I'd be happy to have him there with Teenie and me and Mary Hannah.

We found Teenie in the kitchen. On the table were dishes of cornbread, light bread, slaw, cucumber pickle, ham, and pork tenderloin, accompanied by at least seven pies. The room smelled of all these things, as well as Dice Cody's old coat, hanging inside the door. I recognized another odor from when Papa's cousin Charlie Wister died.

At the little four-eyed cookstove, Teenie poured out coffee from a blue graniteware pot. She and Joe and I were just dragging our chairs up to the table when Mr. Dave Morgan came stumping in from the back porch. He brought the strong odor of barn with him. I'd never seen Mary Hannah's father, but I recognized him for a Morgan. He looked so much like Mr. Charley Morgan, who lived on the farm below Joe's, that I'd never have mistaken him.

"Dice turned in, I reckon," Mr. Morgan said. "I shut up his stock." He tramped on through the front of the house, and soon, I heard the scrape of a chair overhead and the creak of bedcords.

Teenie loosened the drawstring of a linen bag she'd brought with her and pulled out a small hard-rubber shuttle and a length of tatting.

Over her ball of cotton, she looked at Joe and me. "At nine o'clock, we have to change the cloth."

What cloth? I wondered. As a married woman, Teenie knew things I didn't. She could help lay out a body. I rummaged in my sewing basket for the pillow sham Mama wanted me to hem. I licked the end of my thread, passed it through a needle, and knotted it. Beside the table, on a wooden stand, stood a small bottle, a tin pitcher, and a shallow agateware basin, with some folded cloths. Likely, that was the cloth Teenie meant.

The night before, Mary Hannah had been alive. She might have sat in the chair I sat in. She'd eaten off this table. I'd seen her—a lean, black-haired woman, newly married to Dice—two or three times. Now she was dead, and here Joe and Teenie and I were, drinking coffee out of her cups.

Moth millers the size of nickels struck the lamp's chimney, and the light flickered as they fell sizzling into the flame. Joe patted his pocket for his Zane Gray book.

Teenie checked her watch and frowned. "It's nine o'clock," she said, and laid down her tatting.

Teenie unfolded a cloth from the pile on the wooden stand, shook it out, and spread it in the bottom of the basin. She added water, then uncorked the bottle, and shook a few drops onto the cloth. The familiar odor of carbolic acid filled the air.

Carrying the basin, Teenie went first, Joe followed with the lamp, and I brought up the rear. We made our way down the hall. Snoring came from one of the rooms. It must have been Dice Cody. I'd seen him, too, once or twice. A small, nervous man, he was no kin to me, even if he did have the same name as Mama's father. His Codys came from Hampshire County.

As we entered the front room, an unpleasant odor reminded me of when our mare Kate died. A second lamp showed a woman's body lying on a cot in front of an open window. Newspapers were spread between her and the cot and under the cot. She wore a dark-blue dress. Joe held his lamp high, and Teenie set down her basin. With a deft motion, she swept a cloth off Mary Hannah's face.

Mary Hannah's nose, between the pennies on her eyelids, stuck up like a beak. A cloth tied around the top of her head and her jaw held two pads pressed against her cheeks. Teenie removed the damp cloth from the basin and spread it across Mary Hannah's face. She dropped the used cloth into the basin.

"That keeps her from turning black," Teenie told us in a low voice.

So, that's death, I thought.

I was four when Grandma and Grandpa Wister died, nine the year Dr. Sam and Miss Fanny Hunter lost their fourth baby girl, and twelve when Papa's cousin died of consumption. But I was upset to see the dead body of a woman like Mary Hannah, between my age and Teenie's, not long married, and with a small child.

Now that I was aware of Dice's snoring, I couldn't put it out of my mind. I believed I heard it, faint and far away, like someone sawing lumber out by the barn.

A spiral of flypaper tacked to the low kitchen ceiling hung in the still air. Teenie tossed the used cloth into a bucket, then slid it's wooden lid over the top. She wiped her hands on her apron.

"We have to change it again at eleven," she whispered. "Pie?" she asked.

Joe and I shook our heads.

I dipped up water from the little stove's reservoir into a dishpan, added soft soap from a can, and washed our coffee cups.

"There's a breeze," Joe said. I felt it, too, from the open kitchen door.

Our second trip, at eleven, began like the first. The breeze came in gusts that set the kitchen door swinging and made the flypaper spiral sway. As Teenie dribbled carbolic acid over her second cloth, a door banged shut upstairs.

In the flickering light of Joe's lamp, our shadows jumped as the three of us again made our way down the hall.

Joe lifted his lamp while Teenie wiped away a thread of secretion that glistened in the corner of Mary Hannah's mouth.

How calm Teenie was! I thought.

As if sorting washing in her own kitchen, she flipped the used cloth into the basin. She seemed a lifetime older than I.

Then the hall door clapped shut and both lamps blew out.

In the blackness, my heart drummed. I heard Joe fumble for a match and the scratch of phosphorous. The yellow flame lit up his intent, serious expression. With a click, he set the lamp chimney back into its prongs. Glancing up, his gray eyes gave me a startled look, as if only just discovering I was there.

"Come on," he whispered.

Back in the kitchen, Teenie dropped her basin with a clatter. I saw that she, too, was flustered. I'd believed she was like Joe's mother, one of those people others turned to in emergencies.

The wind made a brushing sound in the trees and batted the kitchen door.

Joe winked at me and then turned to Teenie. "Teenie, did you ever hear about the ghost at Nellie's family's place?"

"That's just a loose board the wind gets hold of, Joe," I said, and heard the ashes collapse in the firebox of the little stove.

Teenie frowned. "I don't believe in ghosts."

Just then, I heard a murmur of voices in the yard and footsteps on the porch.

"It's twelve o'clock," Teenie said, and rolled up her tatting.

Mrs. Righter's sturdy, familiar figure appeared in the doorway. Behind her, against the darkness of the porch, I saw Miss Fan's hired girl. Mrs. Righter's kindly, faded eyes surveyed the three of us. She looked from the basin, to the cloths, to the bottle, and then back at our faces.

"How's everything?"

"You have to change the cloth at one o'clock, Mrs. Righter," Teenie said.

"Law, child, *I* know that."

I felt very close to Mrs. Righter. Her small farm, up the road from ours, was where Mama sent us in any emergency, saying, "Go get Mrs. Righter."

She moved the coffee pot from the back of the stove onto an eye. Miss Fan's hired girl unfolded her apron. Teenie, Joe, and I gathered up our things. On the porch, the breeze cooled my face and throat. Mary Hannah had walked, carried water, and churned butter on those splintery, old boards.

Dice would find another beaky-nosed woman to cook and clean for him. Soon, when people said the name Mary Hannah Cody, not many would remember who she was.

I would remember and so would Joe and Teenie. I knew we'd see ourselves carrying the lamp down that hall. We'd hear Dice snoring and the wind roaming around in the yard outside. We'd see Mary Hannah's nose, dark in spite of all the cloths.

The next day, Mary Hannah's coffin would straddle two chairs in that hall, and Dice's black eyes would dart around to see who had come. While someone nailed her coffin shut, maybe her little boy would creep out to the file of buggies, wagons, and automobiles waiting in the yard. He'd climb up onto a running board, then onto a seat, and turn the steering wheel in his little hands, pretending to drive.

Light, flooding out from Mary Hannah's kitchen, showed Joe bent over the crank of the Ford. Beside him, it lit the moving leaves of a new little tree and the circle of raw ground under it, still wet from Mary Hannah's watering. I heard the Ford's engine catch and felt Teenie's hand touch mine.

"I'll just never, never forget you two staying with me tonight, Nellie," Teenie whispered.

BEN MOOMAW

One warm September forenoon in 1918 Papa sat on the porch of Mrs. Crigler's hotel in Minerva, West Virginia. He was waiting to be called to dinner, after which he intended to stop by the tannery and the bank. He was reading an article in the local newspaper about a young man who had received a degree in land management at the state university.

What was "land management?"

Papa managed a good-sized farm, which his father had managed before him.

"Mr. Wister, may I speak with you?" There stood the subject of the article—Ben Moomaw.

My brother Dayton was fighting in France. Ben's father, a local doctor, had arranged for him to be deferred from military service.

Papa's father had once operated a general store. Ben's costume reminded him of the drummers who tried to sell their wares. He wore a narrow gray suit with a crisp, white shirt and carried a carefully creased black fedora. He drew out one of Mrs. Crigler's hide- bottomed chairs and sat down next to Papa. Ben's family had moved to Minerva from Monterey, Virginia. Papa remembered seeing Ben, a puny child, wearing the long muslin dress of that time and a timorous expression.

"A progressive farmer like you, Mr. Wister, knows more about farming than I ever will," he said. "But have you heard yet about these new commercial fertilizers?"

Papa was annoyed that he'd allowed Ben to corner him. Ben's father had once taken a piece of bottomland in payment from old Mr. Byrd for delivering a grandson.

He said shortly, "I know that land your father got from the Byrds. Anything will grow on it, no matter what you dress it with—horse manure or hog slops or gunpowder. Virgin land doesn't need any help."

The street below Mrs. Crigler's porch was deserted. Nobody was out at Mr. Eddie Sanderson's General Store or at Johnson's Drugstore.

Papa said, "Some of the little places up in the ridges around here could maybe use your fertilizer. Good day." Papa got to his feet and started to head for the dining room.

Ben, like any drummer worth his salt, had the last word. "All the same, sir, it's possible you have a little field somewhere that's not doing as well as you'd like. You might want to call me about it." With that, he gave Papa his card.

By the time Papa arrived home and took care of his horse, it was dark. Mama watched him eat the fried ham, butterbeans, and cornbread she'd kept hot.

She said, "Jack, what is it?"

"Did you read that write-up in this week's *Guthrie County Review* about Doc Moomaw's boy getting a degree in 'land management'?" he asked.

"I saw it. What about it?"

"He tried to tell me I ought to use some of these new fertilizers. Ha! The day I take advice from Doc Moomaw's boy..." His voice trailed off.

Mama smiled. Ben was shrewd to call Papa "progressive." One of Papa's most remarkable traits was his ambition to be the first in everything. He put rubber tires on our buggies, he brought running water into our house and built an indoor bathroom, he replaced our old step-top stove with a modern wood-burning range, and he installed an electricity-generating system.

The only ones who beat Papa at anything were Mama's father and, sometimes, her brother Virgil. He owned the first automobile and the biggest barn in the valley.

Mama said, "I'm thinking of that field between us and Mrs. Righter." It was twenty-odd acres, where Papa had tried corn, wheat, potatoes, beets, and sorghum. Nothing had ever flourished there.

The next morning, she glanced out the window and saw Papa standing in the corn stubble in that very field. She watched him scoop up a fistful of dirt and weigh it in his cupped palm. Then he dusted off his hands and climbed over the fence to walk slowly toward the house.

In October, he walked there again. After the men plowed and brought the horses to the barn, he went to meet them.

"I want you to plow that field again," Papa said. "But before you do, spread some of this new fertilizer on it."

Ben Moomaw delivered the fertilizer. The men spread and plowed it in. One strip, close to Mrs. Righter's little house, they left untreated. They planted the field with wheat.

Soon, the crop was up. Where the new fertilizer had been spread, the foliage was a darker green and the plants taller and stouter than those growing in the unfertilized section.

Papa made special trips to inspect the wheat in our end of the field, then at the end next to Mrs. Righter's house.

One day, Mama threw on a shawl and joined him.

"Wait till Pa sees this, Jack!" she said. "Wait till Virgil gets a look at this!"

Fall advanced into winter. The difference increased between the two ends of the field. Harvesting the crop, our men set aside the grain to be weighed separately. Not only were the kernels bigger and heavier, but there were also more of them per acre.

The following spring, Papa spread Ben Moomaw's fertilizer on all our fields, with the usual quantity of manure. Our crops were better than ever.

Mama had the new fertilizer spread on the vegetable garden, and in time, our neighbors were doing the same. Soon, nobody thought anything special about using commercial fertilizers. Old timers, though, remembered when Jack Wister was the first to use them.

In Flanders, my brother Dayton was injured by mustard gas. He came home in pretty good shape, wearing a decoration for valor.

Ben never married. After Dr. Moomaw died, he continued to live with his mother in the family house. He never stopped experimenting on the bit of land his father had left him. With Papa's approval, he continued to bring prospective customers to look at our farm. When the Second World War broke out, Ben made a great thing of getting his nephews exempted from the draft. I don't remember if he claimed they had bad hearts or asthma. Ever the drummer, ever the salesman, Ben was not admired or even liked in our community.

OTIS AND DORSEY SMUCKER

The sight of Otis Smucker shuffling up our farm lane meant spring had come. Otis lived in Cuyler, a community settled by Lutherans. They built sturdy houses, big barns, and strong split-rail fences. But there was nothing sturdy or well built about Otis.

Skinny and stooped, he rode a swaybacked old mare. Mama said a good wind could have blown them right off the mountain.

Upon his arrival, he greeted us children. "How do, little miss? How do, young fellers? I have business with yer pa."

Papa sat on the porch with Otis and asked him about the winter in Cuyler: Who had married? Who had died? Otis answered these questions, then got around to business.

"What's yer opinion of these here new tooth harrows? I hear tell they're good on stumpy ground."

Papa agreed that tooth harrows were good on stumpy ground. He agreed to lend Otis seventeen dollars to buy one. In 1904, seventeen dollars could buy a first-rate shotgun, a six-burner cook stove, a hundred-and-fifty-piece set of Johnson Brothers chinaware, or a matched set of plush-upholstered, solid-oak parlor furniture.

Next, Otis said he had a pair of spring lambs to sell. Papa agreed to buy them, then invited him to dinner.

Otis never uttered a word during dinner. Afterward, jingling the money in his pocket, he mounted his old mare for the ride back to Cuyler.

Otis had a brother named Dorsey, a glum old codger who wore a red bandanna tied over his ears, with a misshapen felt hat over it. Unlike Otis, he didn't acknowledge our presence.

When Dorsey arrived, without so much as a glance in our direction, he announced, "I come to see yer pa." With that, he made his way around the big limestone chimney to the porch.

Papa sat with Dorsey on the porch and asked how things had been over the winter in Cuyler.

"Poorly, Mr. Wister, poorly," Dorsey answered. He then told of the ailments he'd suffered: rheumatism, toothache, cramp colic, dropsy, lumbago, pleurisy, asthma, neuralgia, inflammation of the bowel, fever sores, corns, ingrown toenails, and warts.

He'd cured his warts, he said, by washing them in water from an elm stump in the dark of the moon. He'd cured a bout of rheumatism by cutting a two-inch plug out of a big white oak tree and burying three of his hairs in the hole.

My brother Dayton told Dorsey that he suffered from a crooked toe. Dorsey closed his eyes, passed his hands over Dayton, and declared that the crooked toe would be straight by the time the moon pointed up. Dayton gleefully declared that his toe would always be crooked, as that was the nature of toes.

Dorsey was so offended that he left without waiting to talk further with Papa. Six years later, he came back, but refused to talk about his ailments, despite Papa's considerable efforts to draw him out.

One day, Mama was entertaining three of her female friends when a knock came at the door. A nicely dressed and very good-looking young man asked to see Papa. He said he was Sawyer Smucker and that Papa had lent him money to pay his fees at the state normal school at Shepherdstown. She said Papa wasn't home, but asked him to join her and her friends in the parlor.

A few days later, Sawyer came back. He told Papa he'd like to "call on Miss Ivy." She was the youngest of Mama's three guests. By then, Mama had figured out that he was a son of Otis Smucker.

Miss Ivy and Sawyer were married in our parlor. Papa sent our hired man with a buggy to bring the wives of Otis and Dorsey to the ceremony. Otis's wife was an interesting woman, but Dorsey's was as dull as Dorsey himself.

Within a year, Ivy and Sawyer had twin boys, whom they named for their father and uncle. Papa made Sawyer an officer of a small bank he controlled. Under Papa's tutelage, Sawyer bought land and became a justice of the peace. The United States entered World War I, and Sawyer volunteered for the Army. He was killed in France.

His widow asked Papa to help compose an obituary. "Squire Sawyer, Guthrie County's Foremost Citizen," she wrote. Papa thought her words excessive, but he couldn't blame her. She concluded, "His ancestors were common folk of gentle grace and dignity."

A picture I have of Papa in the 1930s shows him sitting on the porch in his favorite green rocking chair. His hair is thin and white, and his hands are folded on the head of a cane. On either side of him sit Dorsey, with his battered old hat and bandanna, and Otis Smucker.

Papa on Fred in front of our house

ALWAYS WELCOME,
ALWAYS PLENTY:
AN EPILOGUE

I always believed the way we lived, with so many different characters descending on us, was how everyone lived. I began to suspect otherwise when one day at my friend Maud Flood's house I heard her mother say sharply, "Go on to the next place, *they*'ll take you in!" A ragged man then left her doorway and headed up the road toward our house. Another neighbor nailed a sign to her gate, "TRAVELERS REST," but no traveler ever stopped there. Every traveler who came through our valley knew we took in everyone, fed them and charged nothing.

One rainy night around 1904 Papa was working at his desk when he happened to look out the window. He saw a tiny light in the field below the road. It glimmered briefly in the darkness then winked out. Papa dragged up the sash to get a better look but all he got was a face full of rain and blowing leaves.

Mama was with us children in the sitting room. Our newest baby sister was asleep in the trundle bed. The hall door burst open. There stood Papa.

"Somebody's trying to light a fire down in the field," he announced, shrugging into an oilskin and tossing one to my brother. "Dayton, bring a lantern."

"Oh dear," Mama sighed, "let's get ready." I understood that Papa was setting off to rescue some poor tramp from the rainy dark.

In the kitchen Mama raked up the embers in our big wood-burning range. I brought milk and leftover light-bread from the pantry. From the back of the pantry door I unhooked a tin bathtub.

In the sitting room, Mama and I sorted through the old-clothes basket for a warm union suit, a woolen shirt and pants, a sweater and vest, socks and a pair of resoled shoes.

We had carried these things to the kitchen when a scraping of boots resounded on the porch, the door burst open and a gust of rain swept in bringing Papa, Dayton and an old man bundled in streaming rags.

"This is Mr. Johnson," Papa told us. "*Amos* gave him *raw potatoes.*"

In Papa's voice I heard, not for the first time, his scorn for a neighbor who had given a hungry man raw potatoes and turned him away on a stormy night.

"My boy here will take your wet things, Mr. Johnson," Papa said.

A powerful odor blossomed in the warm room. As Dayton and I headed up to bed he gasped *"Phew!"* He held his nose. *"Peee-eeew!"*

The next morning a small, clean, rosy-cheeked old man joined us at breakfast. Smelling powerfully of lye soap, he looked so different from the half-drowned apparition of the night before it was hard to believe he could be the same.

He never stopped talking. "The older I git the more partial I am to the road," he said, helping himself to biscuits and damson jam. "My oldest girl she's always a-going on at me about moving in with her but I don't keer for the settled life. Weather don't bother me one iota." He prattled on. Papa looked amused. Mama looked resigned.

Mr. Johnson left us wearing Papa's old overcoat and hat and Grandpa Wister's knitted scarf. He carried a big chunk of cornbread and a thick slice of home-cured ham. Dayton used two sharp sticks to jab up his rags and nudge them out to the washhouse for our washerwoman to deal with.

"Do you think anyone ever treated that old man as well as we did?" Mama said. I then understood what it meant to be married to a man like my father who invited all comers. "Always welcome, always plenty," my father unfailingly said to anyone he met.

"Let's see what we have now," Mama said, drawing the old-clothes basket near. "Your Papa will want us to be ready for the next one that comes along."